ACCIDENTAL HERO

Born In Texas: Hometown Heroes A-Z, Book #1

JO GRAFFORD

Copyright © 2021 by Jo Grafford

All rights reserved.

No part of this book may be reproduced in any form or by any electronic or mechanical means, including information storage and retrieval systems, without written permission from the author, except for the use of brief quotations in a book review.

ISBN: 978-1-944794-82-8

ACKNOWLEDGMENTS

An enormous thank you to my editor, Cathleen Weaver! Plus, another big thank you goes to my most faithful beta reader, Mahasani. I also want to give a shout out to my Cuppa Jo Readers on Facebook. Thank you for reading and loving my books!

Join Cuppa Jo Readers at https://www.facebook.com/groups/CuppaJoReaders for sneak peeks, cover reveals, book launches, birthday parties, giveaways, and more!

Free Book!

Also, visit www.JoGrafford.com to sign up for Jo's New Release Newsletter and receive your FREE copy of one of her sweet and clean romance stories!

ABOUT THIS SERIES

Born In Texas: Hometown Heroes A-Z is a sweet and inspirational series of standalone romance stories about small town, everyday heroes. Each title is full of faith and family, hope and love, and always ends in a happily-ever-after!

TITLES:
Accidental Hero
Best Friend Hero

Celebrity Hero
Damaged Hero
Enemies to Hero
Forbidden Hero
Guardian Hero
Hunk and Hero
Instantly Her Hero
Jilted Hero
Kissable Hero
Long Distance Hero
Mistaken Hero
Not Good Enough Hero
Opposites Attract Hero
Playboy Hero
Quiet & Shy Hero
Rockstar Hero
Second Chance Hero
Tortured Hero
Undercover Hero
Volunteer Hero
Workplace Hero
XOXO Hero
Yours Forever Hero
Zillionaire Hero

CHAPTER 1: PILE UP

Matt

I can't believe I fell for her lies!

Feeling like the world's biggest fool, Matt Romero gripped the steering wheel of his white Ford F-150. He was cruising up the sunny interstate toward Amarillo, where he had an interview in the morning; but he was arriving a day early to get the lay of the land. Well, that was partly true, anyway. The real reason he couldn't leave Sweetwater, Texas fast enough was because *she* lived there.

It was one thing to be blinded by love. It was another thing entirely to fall for the stupidest line in a cheater's handbook.

Cat sitting. I actually allowed her to talk me into cat sitting! Or house sitting, which was what it actually amounted to by the time he'd collected his fiancée's mail and carried her latest batch of Amazon deliveries inside. All of that was in addition to feeding and watering her cat and scooping out the litter box.

It wasn't that he minded doing a favor now and then for the woman he planned to spend the rest of his life with. What he minded was that she wasn't in New York City doing her latest modeling gig, like she'd claimed. *Nope.* Nowhere near the Big Apple. She'd been shacked up with another guy. In town. Less than ten miles away from where he'd been cat sitting.

To make matters worse, she'd recently talked Matt into leaving the Army — for her. Or *them*, she'd insisted. A bittersweet decision he'd gladly made, so they could spend more quality time together as a couple. So he could give her the attention she wanted and deserved. So they could have a real marriage when the time came.

Unfortunately, by the time he'd finished serving his last few months of duty as an Army Ranger, she'd already found another guy and moved on. She hadn't even had the decency to tell him! If it wasn't for her own cat blowing her cover, heaven only knew when he would've found out about her unfaithfulness. Two days before their wedding, however, on that fateful cat sitting mission, Sugarball had knocked their first-date picture off the coffee table, broken the glass, and revealed the condemning snapshot his bride-to-be had hidden beneath the top photo. One of her and her newest boyfriend.

And now I'm single, jobless, and mad as a—

The scream of sirens jolted Matt back to the present. A glance in his rearview mirror confirmed his suspicions. He was getting pulled over. *For what?* A scowl down at his speedometer revealed he was cruising at no less than 95 mph. *Whoa!* It was a good twenty miles over the posted speed limit. *Okay, this is bad.* He'd be lucky if he didn't lose his license over this — his fault entirely for driving distracted without his cruise control on. *My day just keeps getting better.*

Slowing and pulling his truck to the shoulder, he coasted to a stop and waited. And waited. And waited some more. A peek at his side mirror showed the cop was still sitting in his car and talking on his phone. *Give me a break.*

To ease the ache between his temples, Matt reached for the red cooler he'd propped on the passenger seat and dragged out a can of soda. He popped the tab and tipped it up to chug down a much-needed shot of caffeine. He hadn't slept much the last couple of nights. Sleeping in a hotel bed wasn't all that restful. Nor was staying in a hotel in the same town where his ex lived. His very public figure of an ex, whose super-model figure appeared in all too many commercials, posters, magazine articles, and online gossip rags.

Movement in his rearview mirror caught his attention. He watched as the police officer finally opened his door, unfolded his large frame from the front seat of his black SUV, and stood. But he continued talking on his phone. *Are you kidding me?* Matt swallowed a dry chuckle and took another swig of his soda. It was a good thing he'd hit the road the day before his interview at the Pantex nuclear plant. The way things were going, it might take the rest of the day to collect his speeding ticket.

By his best estimate, he'd reached the outskirts of Amarillo, maybe twenty or thirty miles out from his final destination. He'd already passed the exit signs for Hereford. Or the beef capital of the world, as the small farm town was often called.

He reached across the dashboard to open his glove compartment and fish out his registration card and proof of insurance. There was going to be no talking his way out of this one, unless the officer happened to have a soft spot for soldiers. He seriously doubted any guy in blue worth his spit would have much sympathy for someone going twenty miles over the speed limit, though.

Digging for his wallet, he pulled out his driver's license. Out of sheer habit, he reached inside the slot where he normally kept his military ID and found it empty. *Right.* He no longer possessed one, which left him with an oddly empty feeling.

He took another gulp of soda and watched as the officer finally pocketed his cell phone. *Okay, then. Time to get this party started.* Matt chunked his soda can in the nearest cup holder and stuck his driver's license, truck registration, and insurance card between two fingers. Hitting an automatic button on the door, he lowered his window a few inches and waited.

The guy heading his way wore the uniform of a Texas state trooper — blue tie, tan Stetson pulled low over his eyes, and a bit of a swagger as he strode to stand beside Matt's window.

"License and registration, soldier."

Guess I didn't need my military ID, after all, to prove I'm a soldier. An ex soldier, that is. Matt had all but forgotten about the Ranger tab displayed on his license plate. He wordlessly poked the requested items through the window opening.

"Any reason you're in such a hurry this morning?" the officer mused in a curious voice as he glanced over Matt's identification. He was so tall, he had to stoop to peer through the window. Like Matt, he was tan, brown haired, and sporting a goatee. However, the officer was a good several inches taller.

"Nothing worth hearing, officer." *My problem. Not yours. Don't want to talk about it.* Matt squinted through the glaring sun to read the guy's name on his tag. *McCarty*.

"Yeah, well, we have plenty of time to chat, since this is going to be a hefty ticket to write up." Officer McCarty's tone was mildly sympathetic, though it was impossible to read his expression behind his sunglasses. "I clocked you going twenty-two miles over the posted limit, Mr. Romero."

Twenty-two miles? Not good. Not good at all. Matt's jaw tightened, and he could feel the veins in his temples throbbing. Looked like he was going to have to share his story, after all. Maybe, just maybe, the trooper would feel so sorry for him that he'd give him a warning. It was worth a try, anyway. *If nothing else, it'll give you something to snicker about over your next coffee break.*

"Today was supposed to be my wedding day." He spoke through stiff lips, finding a strange sort of relief in confessing that sorry fact to a perfect stranger. Fortunately, they'd never have to see each other again.

"I'm sorry for your loss." Officer McCarty glanced up from Matt's license to give him what felt like a hard stare. Probably trying to gauge if he was telling the truth or not.

Matt glanced away, wanting to set the man's misconception straight but not wishing to witness his pity when he did. "She's still alive," he muttered. "Found somebody else, that's all." He gripped the steering wheel and drummed his thumbs against it. *I'm just the poor sap she lied to and cheated on heaven only knew how many times.*

He was so done with women, as in never again going to put his heart on the chopping block of love. *Better to live a lonely life than to let another person destroy you like that.* She'd taken everything from him that mattered — his pride, his dignity, and his career.

"Ouch!" Officer McCarty sighed. "Well, here comes the tough part about my job. Despite your reasons, you were shooting down the highway like a bat out of Hades, which was putting lives at risk. Yours, included."

"Can't disagree with that." Matt stared straight ahead, past the small spidery nick in his windshield. He'd gotten hit by a rock earlier while passing a semi tractor trailer. It really hadn't been his day. Or his week. Or his year, for that matter. It didn't mean he was going to grovel, though. The guy might as well give him his ticket and be done with it.

A massive dump truck on the oncoming side of the highway abruptly swerved into the narrow, grassy median. It was a few hundred yards or so away, but his front left tire dipped down, *way* down, and the truck pitched heavily to one side.

"Whoa!" Matt shouted, pointing to get Officer McCarty's attention. "That guy's in trouble!"

Two vehicles on their side of the road passed their parked vehicles in quick succession. A rusted blue van pulling a fifth wheel and a shiny red Dodge Ram. New looking.

Matt laid on his horn to warn them, just as the dump truck started to roll. It was like watching a horror movie in slow motion, knowing something bad was about to happen while being helpless to stop it.

The dump truck slammed onto its side and skidded noisily across Matt's lane. The blue van whipped to the right shoulder in a vain attempt to avoid a collision. Matt winced as the van's bumper caught the hood of the skidding dump truck nearly head on, then jack-knifed into the air like a gigantic inchworm.

The driver of the red truck was only a few car lengths behind, jamming so hard on its brakes that it left two dark smoking lines of rubber on the pavement. Seconds later, it careened into the median and flipped on its side. It wasn't immediately clear if the red pickup had collided with any part of the dump truck. However, an ominous swirl of smoke seeped from its hood.

For a split second, Matt and Officer McCarty stared in shock at each other. Then the officer shoved his license and registration back through the opening in the window. "Suddenly got better things to do than give you a ticket." He sprinted for his SUV, leaped inside, and gunned it around Matt with his sirens blaring and lights flashing. He drove a short distance and stopped with his vehicle canted across both lanes, forming a temporary blockade.

Matt might no longer be in the military, but his protect-and-defend instincts kicked in. There was no telling how long it could take the emergency vehicles to arrive, and he didn't like the way the red pick up was smoking. The driver hadn't climbed out of the cab which wasn't a good sign.

Officer McCarty reached the blue van first, probably because it was the closest, and assisted a dazed man from one of the back passenger doors. He led the guy to the side of the road, helped him get seated on a small incline, then jogged back to help the next passenger exit the van. Unfortunately, Officer McCarty was only one man, and this was much bigger than a one-man job.

Following his gut, Matt flung off his emergency brake and gunned his motor up the shoulder, pausing a few car lengths back from the collision. Turning off his motor, he leaped from his truck and jogged across the double lane to the red pickup. The motor was still running, and the smoke was rising more thickly now.

Holy snap! Whoever was in there needed to get out immediately before it caught fire or exploded. Arriving at the suspended tailgate of the doomed truck, he took a flying leap and nimbly scaled the cab to reach the driver's door. Unsurprisingly, it was locked.

Pounding on the window, Matt shouted at the driver. "You okay in there?"

There was no answer and no movement. Peering closer, he could make out the still form of a woman. Blonde, pale, and curled to one side. The only thing holding her in place was the snarl of a seatbelt around her waist. A trickle of red ran across one cheek.

Matt's survival training kicked in. Crouching over the side of the truck, he quickly assessed the damage to the windshield and decided it wasn't enough to make it the best entry point. *Too bad.* Because his only other option was to shower the driver with glass. *Sorry, lady!* Swinging a leg, he jabbed the back edge of his boot heel into the edge of the glass, nearest the lock. His luck held when he managed to pop a fist-sized hole instead of shattering the entire pane.

Reaching inside, he unlocked the door and pulled it open. The next part was a little trickier, since he had to reach down, *way* down, to unbuckle the woman and catch her weight before she fell. It would've been easier is she was conscious and able to follow instructions. Instead, he was going to have to rely on his many years of physical training.

I can do this. I have to do this. An ominous hiss of steam and smoke from beneath the front hood stiffened his resolve and made him move faster.

"Come on, lady," Matt muttered, releasing her seatbelt and catching her. With a grunt of exertion, he hefted her free of the mangled cab. Then he half-slid, half hopped to the ground with her in his arms and took off at a jog.

Clad in jeans, boots, and a pink and white plaid shirt, she was lighter than he'd been expecting. Her upper arm, that his left hand was cupped around, felt desperately thin despite her baggy shirt. It was as if she'd recently been ill and lost a lot of weight. One long, strawberry blonde braid dangled over her shoulder, and a sprinkle of freckles stood out in stark relief against her pale cheeks.

He hoped like heck she hadn't hit her head too hard on impact. Visions of various traumatic brain injuries and their various complications swarmed through his mind, along with the possibility he'd just moved a woman with a broken neck. *Please don't be broken.*

Since the road was barricaded, he carried the woman to the far right shoulder and up a grassy knoll where Officer McCarty was depositing the other injured victims. A dry wind gusted, sending a layer of fine-grain dust in their direction, along with one prickly, rolling tumbleweed. About twenty yards away was a rocky canyon wall that went straight up, underscoring the fact that there really hadn't been any way for the hapless van and pickup drivers to avoid the collision. They'd literally been trapped between the canyon and oncoming traffic.

An explosion ricocheted through the air. Matt's back was turned to the mangled pile of vehicles, but the blast shook the ground beneath him. On pure instinct, he dove for the grass, using his body as a shield over the woman in his arms. He used one hand to cradle her head against his chest and his other to break their fall as best as he could.

A few people cried out in fear, as smoke billowed around them, blanketing the scene. For the next few minutes, it was difficult to see much, and the wave of ensuing heat had a suffocating feel to it. The woman beneath Matt remained motionless, though he was pretty sure she mumbled something a few times. He crouched over her, keeping her head cradled beneath his hand. A quick exam determined she was breathing normally, but she was still unconscious. He debated what to do next.

The howl of a fire engine sounded in the distance. His shoulders slumped in relief. Help had finally arrived. More sirens blared, and the area was soon crawling with fire engines, ambulances, and paramedics with stretchers. One walked determinedly in his direction through the dissipating smoke.

"What's your name, sir?" the EMT worker inquired in calm, even tones. Her chin-length dark hair was blowing nearly sideways in the wind. She shook her head to knock it away, revealing a pair of snapping dark eyes that were full of concern.

"I'm Sergeant Matt Romero," he informed her out of sheer habit. *Well, maybe no longer the sergeant part.* "I'm fine. This woman is not. I don't know her name. She was unconscious when I pulled her from her truck."

As the curvy EMT stepped closer, Matt could read her name tag. *Corrigan.* "I'm Star Corrigan, and I'll do whatever I can to help." Her forehead wrinkled in alarm as she caught sight of the injured woman's face. "Omigosh! Bree?" Tossing her red medical bag on the ground, she slid to her knees beside them. "Oh, Bree, honey!" she sighed, reaching for her pulse.

"I-I..." The woman stirred. Her lashes fluttered a few times against her cheeks. Then they snapped open, revealing two pools of the deepest blue Matt had ever seen. They held a very glazed-over look in them as they latched onto his face. "Don't go," she pleaded with a hitch to her voice that might've been due to emotion or the amount of smoke she'd inhaled.

Either way, it tugged at every one of his heartstrings. There was a lost ring to her voice, along with an air of distinct vulnerability, that made him want to take her in his arms again and cuddle her close.

"I won't," he promised huskily, hardly knowing

what he was saying. He probably would have said anything to make the desperate look in her eyes go away.

"I'm not loving her heart rate." Star produced a penlight and flipped it on. Shining it in one of her friend's eyes, then the other, she cried urgently, "Bree? It's me, Star Corrigan. Can you tell me what happened, hon?"

A shiver worked its way through Bree's too-thin frame. "Don't go," she whispered again to Matt, before her eyelids fluttered closed. Another shiver worked its way through her, despite the fact she was no longer conscious.

"She's going into shock." Star glanced worriedly over her shoulder. "Need a stretcher over here!" she called sharply. One was swiftly rolled their way.

Matt helped her lift and deposit their precious burden aboard.

"Can you make it to the hospital?" Star asked as he helped push the stretcher toward the nearest ambulance. "Bree seemed pretty intent on having you stay with her."

Matt's brows shot up in surprise. "Uh, sure." As far as he could tell, he'd never laid eyes on the injured woman before today. More than likely she'd mistaken him for someone else. He didn't mind helping out, though. *Who knows?* Maybe he could give her medical team some information about the rescue that they might find useful in her treatment.

Or maybe he was just drawn to the fragile-looking

Bree for reasons he couldn't explain. Whatever the case, he found he wasn't in a terrible hurry to bug out of there. He had plenty of extra time built into his schedule before his interview tomorrow. The only real task he had left for the day was finding a hotel room once he reached Amarillo.

"I just need to let Officer McCarty know I'm leaving." Matt shook his head sheepishly. "I kinda hate to admit this, but he had me pulled over for speeding when this all went down." He waved a hand at the carnage around them. It was a dismal sight of twisted, blackened metal and scorched pavement. All three vehicles were totaled.

Star snickered, then seemed to catch herself. "Sorry. Inappropriate laughter. Very inappropriate laughter."

He shrugged, not in the least offended. A lot of people laughed when they were nervous or upset, which she clearly was about her unconscious friend. "Guess it was pretty stupid of me to be driving these long empty stretches without my cruise control on." Especially with the way he'd been seething and brooding nearly non-stop for the past seventy-two hours.

Star shot him a sympathetic look. "Believe me, I'm not judging. Far from it." She reached out to pat Officer McCarty's arm as they passed him with the stretcher. "The only reason a bunch of us in Hereford don't have a lot more points on our licenses, is because we grew up with this sweet guy."

"Aw, shoot! Is that Bree?" Officer McCarty groaned. He pulled his sunglasses down to take a closer look over the top of them. His stoic expression was gone. In its place was one etched with worry. The personal kind. Like Star, he knew the victim.

"Yeah." Star's pink glossy lips twisted. "She and her brother can't catch a break, can they?"

Since they were only a few feet from the back of an ambulance and since two more paramedics converged on them to help lift the stretcher, Matt peeled away to face the trooper who'd pulled him over.

"Any issues with me following them to the hospital, officer? Star asked if I would." Unfortunately, it would give the guy more time and opportunity to ticket Matt, but that couldn't be helped.

"Emmitt," Officer McCarty corrected. "Just call me Emmitt, alright? I think you more than worked off your ticket back there."

"Thanks, man. Really appreciate it." Matt held out a hand, relieved to hear he'd be keeping his license.

They soberly shook hands, eyeing each other.

"You need me to come by the PD to file a witness report or anything before I boogie out of town?"

"Nah. Just give me a call, and we'll take care of it over the phone." Emmitt pulled out his wallet and produced a business card. "Not sure if we'll need your story, since I saw how it went down, but we should probably still cross every T."

"Roger that." Matt stuffed the card in the back pocket of his jeans.

"Where are you headed, anyway?"

"Amarillo. Got an interview at Pantex tomorrow."

"Solid company." Emmitt nodded. "Got several friends who work up there."

Star leaned out from the back of the ambulance. "You coming?" she called to Matt.

He nodded vigorously and jogged toward his truck. Since the ambulance was on the opposite side of the accident, he turned on his blinker, crossed the lanes near Emmitt's SUV, and put his oversized tires to good use traversing the pitchy median. He had to spin his wheels a bit in the center of the median to get his tires to grab the sandy incline leading to the other side of the highway. Once past the accident, he had to re-cross the median to get back en route. It was a good thing he'd upgraded his truck for off-roading purposes.

They continued north and drove the final twenty minutes or so to Amarillo, which boasted a much bigger hospital than any of the smaller surrounding towns. Luckily, Matt was able to grab a decently close parking spot just as another vehicle was leaving. He jogged into the waiting room, dropped Star Corrigan's name a few times, and tried to make it sound like he was a close friend of the patient. A "close friend" who sadly didn't even know her last name.

The receptionist made him wait while she paged Star, who appeared a short time later to escort him back. "She's in Bay 6," she informed him in a strained voice, reaching for his arm and practically dragging him behind the curtain.

If anything, Bree looked even thinner and more fragile than she had outside on the highway. A nurse was bent over her, inserting an I.V.

"She still hasn't woken up. Hasn't even twitched." Star's voice was soft, barely above a whisper. "They're pretty sure she has a concussion. Gonna run the full battery of tests to figure out what's going on for sure."

Matt nodded, not knowing what to say.

The EMT's pager went off. She snatched it up and scowled at it. "Just got another call. It's a busy day out there for motorists." She punched in a reply, then cast him a sideways glance. "Any chance you can stick around until Bree's brother gets here?"

That's when it hit him that this had been her real goal all along — to ensure that her friend wasn't left alone. She'd known she could get called away to the next job at any second.

"No problem." He offered what he hoped was a reassuring smile. Amarillo was his final destination, anyway. "This is where I was headed, actually. Got an interview at Pantex in the morning."

"No kidding! Well, good luck with that," she returned with a curious, searching look. "A lot of my friends moved up this way for jobs after high school."

Emmitt had said the same thing. "Hey, ah..." He hated detaining her a second longer than necessary, since she was probably heading out to handle another emergency. However, it might not hurt to know a few more details about the unconscious Bree if he was to be left alone with her. "Mind telling me Bree's last name?"

"Anderson. Her brother is Brody. Brody Anderson. They run a ranch about halfway between here and Hereford, so it'll take him a good twenty minutes or so to get here."

"No problem. I can stay. It was nice meeting you, by the way." His gaze landed on Bree's left hand, which was resting limply atop the white blankets on her bed. It was bare of a wedding ring. *Why did I look? I'm a complete idiot for looking.* He forced his gaze back to the EMT. "Sorry about the circumstances, though."

"Me, too." She shot another worried look at her friend and dropped her voice conspiratorially. "Hey, you're really not supposed to be back here since you're not family, but I sorta begged and they sorta agreed to fudge on the rules until Brody gets here." She eyed him worriedly.

"Don't worry." He could tell she hated the necessity of leaving. "I'll stay until he gets here, even if I get booted out to the waiting room with the regular Joes."

"Thanks! Really." She whipped out her cell phone. "Here's my number in case you need to reach me for anything."

Well, that was certainly a smooth way to work a

pickup line into the conversation. Not that Matt was complaining. His sorely depleted ego could use the boost. He dug for his phone. "Ready."

She rattled off her number, and he quickly texted her back so she would have his.

"Take care of her for me, will you, Matt?" she pleaded anxiously.

On second thought, that was real worry in her voice without any trace of a come-on. Maybe Star hadn't been angling for his number, after all. Maybe she was just that desperate to ensure her friend wasn't going to be left alone in the ER. He nodded his agreement and fist-bumped her.

She tapped back, pushed past the curtain, and was gone. The nurse followed, presumably to report Bree's vitals to the ER doctor on duty.

Matt moved to the foot of the hospital bed. "So who do you think I am, Bree?" *Why did you ask me to stay?*

Her long blonde lashes remained resting against her cheeks. It looked like he was going to have to stick around for a while if he wanted answers.

CHAPTER 2: NEW PARTNER

Matt

The nurses and ER doc came and went several times from Bree Anderson's bay, all but ignoring Matt. He overheard something about hurrying up their initial screening so they could get her down to the Radiology Department for x-rays ASAP.

Before they rolled her away, however, a lone cowboy thumped his way into the curtained-off area, leaning heavily on his cane with each step. He limped straight to her side. "Aw, Bree!" he muttered, reaching out to run the back of his hand down the side of her face.

The red had been swabbed off, and a fresh bandage was taped across her cheekbone.

Due to his striking blue gaze, Matt figured he must be in the presence of Brody Anderson. Instead of her strawberry blonde hair, he had a dark buzz cut, almost military in style. He was dressed the same way she was, though, in a plaid shirt, faded jeans, and well-worn boots. Pretty dusty from the ankles down, he looked as if he'd come straight from the fields.

Glancing up from his sister and catching Matt's gaze, Brody extended his hand across the bed. "I'm Brody Anderson. I take it you're the one who pulled her out of her truck?" His jaw was dark with scruff, not enough to call a beard but enough to indicate he normally shaved. He just hadn't gotten around to it during the last day or two.

"I did. Matt Romero here." They shook hands. "I was the lucky guy getting a speeding ticket when it all went down. Since I had a front-row seat, I was able to get there pretty quickly to lend a hand."

"Sorry about the ticket, but I'll confess to being selfishly glad you were there." The cowboy offered him a rueful half-smile. "I'll even help out with the cost of the ticket."

"No need, but thanks." Matt was amazed by the guy's offer. It wasn't the kind of generosity a person ran into often. "Emmitt never got around to writing it. Right after he asked to see my license, that dump truck came careening across the median, flipped over, and..." He paused and shook his head at the horrific memory.

"Well, I can't thank you enough for what you did." Brody wrapped his larger hand around his sister's much smaller one and gently squeezed her fingers. "I'm not sure what all Star told you about us, but Bree is all I have left." For a moment, he looked close to weeping, but he quickly schooled his expression.

"Not too much, actually." Matt was moved by the guy's humble admission, and more curious than ever about his and Bree's story. It was obvious the two siblings were close. Then there was the way both Star and Emmitt had reacted to her injuries. It was beginning to look like there were a lot of people who cared about the unconscious woman on the bed. Matt experienced a curious stab of envy. In comparison, he had nobody. Well, there might as well have been nobody. He had a half-brother named Gabe, but they'd lost touch years ago. Last he'd heard, Gabe was trying to make a go of county singing with some upstart band.

"Star's pretty sweet, isn't she?" Brody asked quietly after a pause. It was an innocuous sounding question, but Matt immediately sensed there was more to it. Something distinctly male and territorial.

He eyed the crippled cowboy, wondering if he and Star had history. "Seems like," he drawled, "But between the accident and the explosion, we didn't exactly have much time to get acquainted. She got called away soon after we arrived at the hospital. Making sure I stayed with your sister until you got here was pretty much the extent of our conversation." Sort of. They'd exchanged phone numbers first, a detail that was beginning to feel less and less relevant.

As Matt described his encounter with Star, Brody seemed to unbend in slow degrees. "Really appreciate that, man." His worried gaze returned to his sister's still form.

A medical assistant in a white smock pulled aside the curtain, making both of them glance up in expectation. "Time to get this lovely lady down to x-ray." His round face lit with a welcoming smile as he nodded at Brody. A lanky fellow with a buzz cut and a full sleeve tattoo on his left arm, he reminded Matt of a medic that had been embedded with his unit during their last deployment. "I take it you're the older brother we've been waiting for?"

"I am." Brody's tanned brow wrinkled as the tech handed him a clipboard with some paperwork to sign. "Anything you can tell me about her condition?"

"She's stable." A man in a white jacket breezed into the bay with his hand outstretched. "I'm Dr. Mulligan." A short and stocky man with silver frost at his temples, he eyed Matt curiously. "Would you care to speak in private?"

Brody followed his gaze. "That won't be necessary. This is the guy who rescued my sister. I'd like to keep him around, if you don't mind, in case you have any questions about what happened, er...that sort of thing."

"It's entirely up to you, Mr. Anderson." The ER doc's gaze narrowed in concern. "As you may have already guessed, your sister is in a coma, which is why we're pushing so hard to get her to x-ray. Normally, we'd invite you to go with her, but they've been pretty over-run the past few hours, so they're asking us to minimize the traffic." He nodded at the medical assistant to get moving. "The scans I've ordered should reveal the underlying cause of her coma. We'll be looking for all the usual stuff — concussions, bleeds, any other signs of head trauma."

Brody's grim expression told Matt that he understood they were most likely dealing with a brain injury. "How long before we can expect her to wake up, sir?"

Dr. Mulligan pressed his hands together beneath his chin as the medical assistant unlocked the wheels on Bree's bed and rolled her from the bay. "It's hard to say, exactly. A coma is the brain's way of shutting down and taking a time out after experiencing head trauma. The good thing is that her vitals are stable right now. The other good thing is that she's been exhibiting some motor function. Curling her fingers now and then, that sort of thing. A very good sign, believe me."

When he paused, Matt offered quietly, "She opened her eyes and said something to me after the explosion. It was right before the ambulance arrived."

"That's good!" the doctor exclaimed, his features lighting with interest. "Another good sign."

"What did she say?" Brody asked quickly.

"Three words. Please don't go." Matt shook his head. "Since we'd never met, I could only assume she'd mistaken me for someone else."

Brody gave him a troubled look that told him he

knew exactly who his sister had mistaken him for. *Interesting.*

Within the hour, Bree was moved to an intensive care unit, where her medical team expected her to remain fully intubated until she awoke.

"Whelp." Brody walked with Matt back to the waiting room. "Guess this means I'll be spending the night. Good thing I came prepared, just in case."

"Is there anything else I can do before I go?" Matt was reluctant to say goodbye. In the short time he'd spent with Brody, they'd chatted up a storm and discovered they had a great deal in common. Not only were they the same age, they shared the same birth month. One of them would turn twenty-seven a few days before Thanksgiving, and the other a few days after. Both of them had also been born and raised in small Texas towns, and both of them had spent a few years in foster care. Unlike Matt, however, Brody and his sister had been adopted by a pair of aging ranchers just north of Hereford. Both had since passed, and the siblings were struggling to run the ranch they'd inherited on their own.

"Now that you mention it? Yeah, there's something else you can do." Brody pushed back his Stetson. "Let me take you to lunch."

Although Matt's stomach was silently howling in hunger, he hesitated, sensing Brody might be short on cash.

Brody sent a light punch to his shoulder. "Oh, come on! It's past noon. There's no way you're not hungry, and it's the least I can do to thank you for everything you've done."

"You're right," Matt relented after a short hesitation. "I'm hungry. Where to?" He'd just have to find a way out of allowing Brody to pick up the tab.

"The hospital cafeteria, dude." Brody grinned. "It's in my price range, and it'll keep us close to Bree. I don't want to be too far away when she wakes up."

When, not if. Matt liked his optimism.

They made their way through the snaking white and chrome hallways to the elevators, which they rode to the Basement level. Since it was nearly one-thirty, the lunch crowd was thinning. Without comparing food preferences, they strolled toward the same food line and found they had yet another thing in common — a love for burgers and fries.

In the end, Matt didn't succeed in picking up his own lunch tab. Brody produced a two-for-one voucher of some sort and managed to purchase both of their lunches for the price of one.

"Thanks for lunch." Matt slid into a corner booth, with his mouth watering over the double burger resting on his tray. Though it was a basement cafeteria without windows, the wide, well-lit room was decked out like an old diner. They were seated on red vinyl benches at a chrome table, with black-and-white checkered tiles at their feet. From a jukebox against the wall, Elvis belted out "A Little Less Conversation."

"Thanks for saving my sister's life," Brody

returned, taking the seat across from him and removing his Stetson. He hooked it on top of his cane, which he propped against the cushion. "That's worth far more to me than a burger. For that, I can never repay you."

Before the conversation got awkward, Matt took a bite and nearly fell into spasms of ecstasy. It was seriously the best hamburger he'd eaten in a long time. Maybe forever. Both burgers were grilled medium well to perfection, with only a hint of pink in their centers.

"So what do you think?"

"What?" Matt stared, wondering why Brody hadn't yet started eating.

"What do you think of the burger?"

Matt was so busy scarfing down another bite that he had to finish chewing and swallowing before answering. "You better either get started on yours or chain it down, man. If you don't, I may have to fight you for it."

Brody burst out laughing. "That's the best compliment I've ever gotten on our brand of beef."

"Your brand?"

Brody's smile dimmed somewhat. "Well, it's not official yet. More like a work in progress."

"So what exactly do you feed your cattle?" Matt waved his burger in the air. "Manna from heaven?"

Brody's dark brows shot up. "You really think it's that good?"

"Eh, Texas boy here, so I know my beef." Matt

placed a hand over his heart. "It's exceptional. How did you do it?"

"It's a family secret, something my adoptive father taught me. What I can tell you is this. It's based on the same concept that bodybuilders and fitness gurus use to sculpt the ideal human physique."

Matt grinned. "Meaning you have the Anderson cows on a special diet." A genius idea, come to think of it.

"A one-of-a-kind diet that I specially produce and grow myself." Brody gave a bittersweet smile that suggested he was recalling times gone by. "Bree used to tease Dad and me about how long we spent working outside in the greenhouses together. Sometimes long after dark by lantern or black light, depending on the experiment. She called it digging in the dirt, as if we were two kids playing outside in the sandbox, instead of pushing the boundaries of horticultural research."

Matt had been eating the whole time Brody was talking, so he was nearly finished with his burger. He eyed the one still sitting on Brody's plate with envy. "Please tell me you've patented your secret formula, and there's a chance I'll be able to buy this stuff soon at a local supermarket." *Good Golly!* Though his belly was nearly full, his mouth was watering at the prospect of getting his hands on some more Anderson brand beef to grill on the back deck. Or back porch. Or back of wherever he ended up living.

Brody's smile disappeared, altogether. "Yeah, that's not going to happen any time soon."

"Why not?" Matt demanded, stuffing his last bite inside his mouth.

"Because it costs money, as in thousands. Eight to ten thousand or more." Brody grimaced. "Thousands I can't currently spare, because—" He stopped in mid-sentence and drew a deep breath. "I was hoping to raise the funds by selling provisional contracts to a few highly vetted vendors, but it hasn't worked out so far."

"Places like this hospital?" Matt's gaze narrowed, as he attempted to put all the pieces together.

"Yeah. I know somebody who knows the manager," Brody explained vaguely. "They all agree it's the best meat they've ever tasted, but nobody wants to pay what it's worth. And if I accept the going rate for regular ol' beef, I'll barely break even." He made a sound of disgust. "I might even lose money."

Matt wasn't normally one to make snap decisions, but he found himself wanting to jump all over the investment opportunity the crippled cowboy had inadvertently laid out before him. Since Matt had never been married and had spent a good amount of the past eight years deployed, he had a decent amount of savings in the bank, plus a thriving mutual fund portfolio. All in all, he was worth a couple hundred grand. He understood a thing or two about risks and returns, and his gut was telling him that investing in Anderson beef was likely to result in a tidy profit.

"What if I front you the money for the patent?" he drawled slowly, still working out the details in his head. If he cashed out a few mutual funds, he could have the money available in three business days.

Brody looked surprised at first, then thoughtful. "Need to ask you something first."

"Yep?" Matt prepared to be bombarded with questions about interest rates and payback terms.

"Do you believe things happen for a reason?"

Not what I was expecting you to ask. "Uh, sure. Like fate?" He failed to see what fate had to do with his offer to pay for a beef patent.

"More like Divine intervention."

Matt blinked. He'd never been much of a religious person. "Maybe, I guess." *Still have no idea what this has to do with my offer to front the money for your patent, but okay.*

Brody gave a faint smile. "Well, it doesn't feel like an accident that you got pulled over for a speeding ticket at just the right time and place to save Bree's life today. Any more than it feels like an accident that you're offering the exact kind of assistance we need to keep from losing our ranch."

"Come again?" Matt laid down the French fry he'd just picked up.

"You heard me," Brody sighed, wearily running a hand through his hair and standing the short tips on end. "I'm already three days late on our mortgage.

Some scholarship Bree thought she had fell through, and I didn't have the heart to tell her we don't have the funds to keep her in college this semester."

Matt snorted but chose to keep his opinions to himself. It was beginning to sound like Brody didn't possess any financial management skills, whatsoever. "So money for the patent isn't going to be enough," he mused.

"Unfortunately, no." Brody pushed his hamburger idly around his plate. "Not your problem, but I trusted the wrong person and let him talk me into a partnership about a year ago. He stuck around just long enough to drain our accounts and break Bree's heart. Then he took off."

"So that's who your sister thought I was?" Matt's gut tightened at the thought. *Her ex?*

"Yeah. You're roughly the same height and build. Considering her head injury, the mistake is understandable."

Matt relieved the poignancy of her words. *Please don't go.* Man, but he understood, all too well, the gut-wrenching sentiment behind those three words. He'd desperately wanted to say the same thing to someone else a few short days ago, but he'd held back. Candy Elliot had sobbed and pleaded with him to give her a second chance, but only after he'd caught her cheating. Remorse wasn't genuine, unless it was freely given. The truth was, she'd already moved on. He needed to do the same.

"You okay over there?" Brody's quiet baritone

broke through Matt's musing. "Didn't mean to weird you out with the fact that you resemble Bree's ex."

"What's his name?" Matt asked suddenly.

Brody's brows lifted in surprise. "Her ex?"

"Yeah."

"Cory Brooks. Why?"

Matt leaned his forearms on the table and met his gaze steadily. "Because I'm not him. Cory Brooks isn't the one offering to pay for your patent. I'm Sergeant Matt Romero, a former Ranger who left the Army for the sole purpose of marrying my girl and spending more time with her. Today was actually supposed to be our wedding day."

"Whoa!" Brody gave a low whistle. "What happened?"

"She couldn't wait. During the few months it took me to finish my military duty, she found somebody else." Matt glanced away as the bitter ache swept him all over again. Betrayal like that had a way of making a person feel worthless. Like nothing. Like less than nothing.

Brody was silent for a moment. When he started speaking again, it was in a disbelieving voice. "So, not only were you right where my sister needed you today, you understood exactly why she begged you to stay." He gave another low whistle. "That's why I believe things happen for a reason."

Matt gave a bark of disbelieving laughter. "Even the bad things?"

Brody shrugged. "If it weren't for the bad things

that happened to you, you wouldn't have been speeding up the highway and getting pulled over right when Bree needed you. If it weren't for my bad things, we wouldn't be sitting here discussing my inability to afford a patent."

And Bree might no longer be alive. *Point taken.* Matt nodded. "You may be on to something," he conceded, though he still wasn't a big fan of bringing faith into the conversation. To him, faith was like rainbows and pixie dust. He was more of a facts and figures kinda guy.

"Agreed. For this reason, I have a different proposition to make to you." Brody's gaze turned calculating. "You need a job, right?"

"That's the plan. My interview at Pantex is in the morning." Not that Matt was desperate or anything. He could afford to live off his safety-net savings for a while if he had to, but finding another job was the wiser decision.

"Pantex is a good company. Great benefits." Brody nodded. "What would you do there?"

"Security." Matt dropped his gaze. "For now." His degree was in Computer Science, but he hadn't taken the time to research any of those positions or draft that kind of resume. He was merely swiping at the low hanging fruit by applying for a job as a security guard. He frowned as he mentally examined his reasons and could only come up with one; he already knew in his gut that his stint in Amarillo would be temporary. Why? His head came up, and his stunned gaze met Brody's, not quite ready to believe in stuff like fate or faith.

"A job in security for now, huh?" Brody gave him a slow, knowing smile. "Doesn't sound like anything permanent."

"It's not. At least not the security part." Maybe the right job at Pantex would work out later on. Maybe it wouldn't. "My degree is actually in computers. Just haven't had the time to do much with it while serving as an Army Ranger." He'd spent the last eight years as a combat arms guy. Frequent deployments. Lots of danger. Plenty of action. Not much time working on a computer.

"What if I said I could give you that chance?" Brody's smile broadened.

"When?" Matt's interest was piqued.

"Right now. Today, in fact." Brody reached inside his pocket and withdrew a set of keys. He worked one off the metal ring and set it on the table between them. "The fact that I trusted the wrong guy and nearly lost my ranch over it, doesn't change the fact that I still need a business partner."

A business partner! Matt blinked. "That sounds like a lot more than an investment in a patent."

"Yep. It's a full-time job, Mr. Romero."

"But I'll be living in Amarillo," Matt protested. Near Pantex, hopefully, which was a good twenty or so miles away.

"Or you could move into our spare cabin on the outer forty." Brody slid the key closer. "Years ago, when he first inherited the property, Pops used it as a hunting cabin. He eventually met and fell in love with Mom. That's when he built the main ranch house, where Bree and I live."

Matt shook his head, hardly able to wrap his brain around what Brody was offering. "What exactly are you asking me to do?"

"Invest in the ranch for a percentage return on profits and the opportunity to apply your computer know-how at running a business. The books. The payroll. The hiring of ranch hands and seasonal workers. All the things that seem to slip and slide under my leadership," he sighed, running a hand through his hair again. "Bree's right. I'd much rather be digging in the dirt."

"So let me get this straight." Matt leaned forward with a chuckle. "You want me to invest in your ranch and take over the running of it in exchange for what? Room and board?" It didn't sound like they were too cash heavy. More like they were living paycheck-to-paycheck with zero savings to fall back on.

"And a percentage in profits with unlimited potential for growth after you help us turn things around." Brody grimaced. "It'll amount to less up front than you were expecting to receive from Pantex, at least during the first few months, but it could amount to a whole lot more later on." He named a percentage and explained how much money Matt could expect to bank every four to six weeks.

Yeah, it was lower than what he was expecting to

get paid as a security guard, but not that much lower, everything considered. And if Brody was serious about throwing in his room and board, that would more than make up for the temporary pay cut.

He met Brody's gaze squarely. "I can't believe I'm saying this, but yes. I'd like to take the job." It was a knee-jerk decision. One he certainly hadn't put much thought into. He'd probably wake up tomorrow regretting it.

"I knew you would." Brody grinned.

"Let me guess," Matt interjected sarcastically, "because it was meant to be?"

"Exactly!" Brody tapped the key. "Take it. The address is 100 Sidewinder Canyon. You can GPS your way there, if you want."

Matt chuckled. "I don't think I'll have any trouble remembering it."

"No one ever does." Brody drummed his fingers on the table. "Feel free to go on down and get settled in. I expect I'll be staying up here a few more days."

Because of Bree. Matt's flash-in-the-bucket elation over the new job opportunity faded a few degrees at the reminder that Brody's sister was still fighting for her life on the floor above them.

"Listen. I, ah..." His mind was already made up about working with the Andersons, but he wasn't one to unnecessarily burn bridges. "I should probably stay the night and show up in person tomorrow morning to cancel things at Pantex. They offered me an interview in good faith. I'd like to thank them for it and explain that something came up with a friend who needs my help more than they do right now."

"I like the fact that you don't intend to leave them hanging." Brody nodded in approval.

Matt was just glad Brody wasn't taking any offense over the fact he was essentially still attending the job interview. "You recommend any particular hotels around here, partner?"

"Yeah. I drove the Anderson horse trailer here. It holds up to five guests, plus six horses.

"Wait a minute. Are you actually inviting me to—"

"Save money while spending a night in a luxury room on wheels?" Brody nodded. "Perks of the new job, man."

CHAPTER 3: HARD REALITIES
Bree

Bree couldn't remember the last time she'd felt so sluggish. And heavy-limbed. And sore. *Oh, my lands!* She nearly moaned out loud from the ache in her head.

"Bree?" a familiar male voice called so urgently that she winced. "Did I imagine it, or did you really move?"

What in the—? It was her brother. She grimaced, wondering why it was so difficult to open her eyes. Clenching her fists, she tried again.

"Can you at least hear me, Bree?"

Her eyelids finally popped open.

"Bree!" he cried in relief, making her wince from the volume of his voice.

"My head hurts." Her voice was so hoarse that she barely recognized it.

To her shock, her words made his blue gaze swim

with tears. It felt like a heavy hand closed around her heart and squeezed.

"Bree," he choked. "You're back."

She blinked in confusion. Why was he crying? He never cried. Something really weird was going on. She struggled to sit up.

"Here. Let me help." Brody hastily tossed his cane aside to grip her shoulders and gently ease her upright. He sat on the edge of the bed for leverage.

She stared around them, amazed at all the antiseptic whiteness. A few beeping and whirring sounds filled her ears. They were definitely not at home. A bruising sensation in her wrist made her glance down. That's when she saw the I.V. Her gaze returned to Brody's. "Why am I in the hospital?" *And why can't I remember coming here?*

He dashed the back of his hand across his eyes. "There was an accident. Do you remember any of it?"

She shook her head, then winced again at the pain the small movement caused. "The last thing I remember is being behind the wheel of my truck." She frowned. "I remember driving through the interchange at Canyon and heading up Highway 27. I was..." her eyes rounded in shock. "I was coming here." She blinked. "To the hospital. Why was I coming to the hospital?" Did she have some debilitating disease that was keeping her from remembering?

"To deliver a batch of Anderson beef to the cafe.

You don't remember?" her brother asked anxiously. "Any of it?"

"No. I'm sorry." Her throat was so dry that she coughed. "Water?" she rasped.

"Got it." He reached for her bed railing and punched one of the buttons on a panel there.

In seconds, a nurse sailed through the door. Her expression brightened at the sight of Bree. "Well, look who's back!" There was genuine gladness in the woman's gaze and no small amount of relief. "I'm Nurse Wimble, by the way. How do you feel?"

"She needs water," Brody explained as she proceeded to tinker with Bree's I.V. bag. Next she examined the machine monitoring her vital signs.

"Coming right up, dear." Nurse Wimble disappeared and returned a few minutes later with a pitcher of ice water and a pair of cups. She rolled a cart away from the wall and set the tray on it. "Your throat may feel dry and scratchy for another day or two," she noted with sympathy. "It's from the breathing tube. It does a great job of maintaining your air supply, but it can give you a doozy of a sore throat."

Breathing tube? Bree reached greedily for the glass of water the nurse poured for her and took a grateful sip. She wasn't really all that thirsty, just desperate to ease the raw sensation in her throat. The icy coolness of the liquid made it doubly soothing.

She sat as still as she could while the nurse checked her pulse rate and looked into her eyes. Her dark hair was speckled with gray and pulled back in a simple bun, giving her a motherly appearance.

"Looking good, Miss Anderson." The nurse stepped back with a pleased expression. "I'll let the doctor know you're awake. He'll be paying you a visit soon."

"Thanks." Bree frowned into her ice cubes as she took another sip. It struck her as odd that the nurse was going to report to her doctor something so mundane as the fact that she was awake. Lowering her glass, she caught her brother's anxious perusal, hating how pale and exhausted he looked. "How long was I out, anyway?"

He drew a rough breath. "Three days. Three of the longest days of my life."

Three whole days? The glass of water trembled in Bree's hand. If she'd been unconscious for that long, that meant... "What's today?" she demanded, wondering why she was having so much trouble remembering such a simple detail.

"Friday."

"Omigosh!" The room tilted dizzily. *I have to get out of here. I have to...* With a huff of exertion, she tried to swing her legs over the side of the bed and nearly toppled to the floor.

"Whoa there, little filly!" Brody caught her and eased her back against the pillows. "Not sure where you think you're going."

"I already missed my Thursday class," she gasped, feeling faint. "I have a research paper due tomorrow, and I…and I…" There was something else nagging at the corner of her mind. Something else she needed to remember that was important, but it remained just out of her reach.

"Don't worry. I called the college and spoke to your instructor," Brody assured in his most annoying why-do-you-continually-doubt-your-brother voice. "A man with a most interesting title, as it turns out. Not mister or doctor, but chef. Apparently, you missed a short quiz on plant-based comfort foods."

Oh. Right. A flood of guilt accompanied his words, as that particular memory came flooding back. Bree had changed her choice of majors a few days ago without informing her brother. Something she had no right to do, considering how many sacrifices he was making to put her through college. Money was tight, and he urgently needed her to improve her business and accounting skills, so she could help out more with running the ranch.

"About that cooking class, Brody." She glanced away, no longer able to meet his eyes.

"Talk to me, Bree."

"I can't do it." She hated the disappointment her words were sure to elicit from him. "I know I should have said something sooner, but I don't think I can spend the rest of my life wading through spreadsheets. I just can't," she repeated, a desperate thread creeping into her voice.

"I know you can't, sis." His voice was grave but

kind. "I reckon I had no right to ask you in the first place."

What? She turned her head so quickly in his direction that the movement made her wince. "You're not upset?"

"Nope. Just sorry I put you through so much unnecessary angst about your college classes. You should've always been free to take the path you were meant to take. Not obligated to take the classes you thought I wanted you to take."

"Oh, come on!" she exploded. "This never had anything to do with what you or I wanted. It's what we need. You *need* me to take math and accounting classes. I know that. I—"

"No longer need you to," he cut in smoothly. "In the time you were under, things have gotten better for us." He smiled. "Promise."

"How?" Her gaze narrowed in suspicion. The last time he claimed he'd made things better, he'd hired Cory Brooks. The man who'd robbed them blind before skipping town. He'd taken far more than their money, too. He'd destroyed her trust, shaken her self confidence, and shattered her heart. She was still picking up the pieces.

"I've hired us a business partner. The right one this time."

Her hands started shaking so badly that she had to return her glass to the cart resting beside her bed. "Listen, Brody, I'll apologize all day long for switching my major to culinary arts without telling you, but that didn't give you any right to..." She ground to a choking halt. "What have you done, Brody?" she wheezed. *What in heaven's name have you gone and done?*

"His name is Matt Romero." Her brother drummed his callused fingers on the food cart. "Former Army Ranger. Really nice guy. I think you'll like him."

You think I'll like him? Bree felt the steam rise from her ears. *Are you kidding me?* How could her brother sit there acting like what he'd done was no big deal?

"Although that all sounds fine and dandy," she spluttered, "how do you know he's even who he says he is?" Pardon the question, but Brody didn't exactly have a great track record for managing human resources. In fact, he might very well be the worst judge of character this side of the Mississippi. He was too nice and too trusting for his own good.

"Don't worry. Emmitt McCarty had him pulled over for speeding right before your accident. He can vouch for the fact that Matt Romero is the real deal. Plus, he has an official Army Ranger tab on his truck plates."

"Speeding, huh?" She latched on to that less-than-desirable detail. "Sounds to me like you hired another lawbreaker."

"Yeah, well, maybe you'll feel differently about his imperfections when I tell you this." Brody's chin came up stubbornly. "He also happens to be the fellow who pulled you from your truck right before the explosion. He risked his life to save yours. That oughta be worth something to you."

Bree briefly closed her eyes. "Of course it is, Brody. Of course it is." He was so hard to argue with when he was in one of his self-righteous moods, but this was serious. She opened her eyes. "I'll tell him myself how grateful I am, but I still fail to see how his heroics in any way qualify him to run a ranch." *Their* ranch. The one they were about to lose if they didn't raise some much-needed cash, and soon.

"You're right. It doesn't. His computer degree does, however. So does his tremendous amount of leadership experience."

So the smooth-talking stranger had a degree, at least. She still didn't like the idea that he'd somehow wormed his way into her brother's good graces while she was unconscious. "Did he grow up on a ranch?" she demanded. "Has he ever worked on one?"

"Nope. He grew up in foster care. Never got adopted. Enlisted in the military the day he turned eighteen."

"Oh, Brody!" she muttered again.

"So here's the deal, sis." Brody set his jaw firmly in his big-brother, no-nonsense way that she found particularly irritating. "You get to keep taking your culinary classes, so long as you help me show him the ropes. It's going to be up to me and you to turn him into a proper ranch manager."

"Me? Seriously, Brody?" Though she occasionally

helped out with the bookkeeping, she spent more time in the kitchen than any other part of the ranch.

"Yes, you," he returned evenly. "Although you enjoy messing with the books less than I do, you're better at it than me. Let's face it, Bree. I'm a farmer, not a businessman. Years ago, when you accused me of being good at one thing, only — digging in the dirt..."

"I was kidding!"

"You were right," he said simply. "Which is why I'm going to need you to throw your full support behind Matt Romero, no matter how tough it may be at first."

"Tough?" She wrinkled her nose at him. "I may have hit my head pretty hard a few days ago, but I don't recall having trouble with my people skills." She got along great with their hired workers, and they'd always treated her with respect in return. That included all four of their full-time employees, along with the steady rotation of part-time and seasonal workers.

"This has nothing to do with your people skills, Bree. Maybe I should just show you what I'm talking about." He pulled his cell phone from his pocket and scrolled through his snapshots. Selecting one, he zoomed in on it. "This is Matt Romero." He held up his phone for her to view the screen.

She froze and reached for his phone. It looked as if Brody had accidentally pulled up a photo of Cory Brooks. "When did you take this picture?"

"This morning," he retorted. "Look again. It's not who you think it is."

Though it made her stomach knot to do so, she forced herself to take another peek at the photo. *Okay. So this Cory look-alike wasn't Cory. He was Matt Romero.* Their new ranch manager. A guy who'd never even attempted to run a ranch before. A guy she was going to be partially responsible for training.

"Do you see the difference now?" her brother prodded.

Bree squinted at the photo again, trying to quell the way it made her heart pound. Same dark hair. Same bronze tan. Same dark eyes. Or maybe not quite the same eyes. Cory's had been more calculating, whereas Matt's were infused with humor. He was either half-squinting at the sun, or Brody had caught him in mid-wink. Unlike Cory, he had facial hair. Not a lot. His short, well-groomed beard was just enough to... Well, just enough.

"Why are you doing this?" she asked faintly.

"Because he's the right person for the job, Bree."

"You felt the same way about Cory."

"I was wrong about Cory, but I'm right about Matt. You'll see."

"Brody," she sighed, handing his phone back.

"What?"

"You're killing me. You're absolutely killing me."

"He can't help the way he looks, Bree. You can't hold it against him."

"I'll try, but it isn't going to be easy." She was

dying on the inside at the thought of having to face Matt Romero every day at work. Why couldn't he have been blonde? Or red-headed? Or tall like Emmitt? Or older like Harley, their most senior employee? She bit her lower lip. He seriously looked enough like Cory to be his brother, or at least a cousin.

"When have you and I ever been faced with easy?" Brody joked.

She glanced around them, feeling stronger with each passing minute. And grimier. She didn't dare give the dusty braid on her shoulder a sniff-test. She could easily tell by the gritty way she felt that she was overdue for a shower. *Oh, golly!*

Brody was watching her closely. "Watcha need, sis?"

"A shower. Then I want to go home." Something she planned to do with or without her doctor's blessing. Where was the blasted guy, anyway? Nurse Wimble had left the room eons ago. One thing was for sure. There was no way Bree was spending one night longer in the hospital while some evil twin of her ex had full run of their ranch.

"That's what I like to hear from my coma patients." A man in a white coat strolled into the room, hands in his pockets.

"Hear what?" she asked irritably, wishing she could reach over and yank her pesky I.V. right out. She hated needles, everything from the sight of them to the feel of them.

"Noise. Words. Questions," he returned cheerfully. "I especially like it when my coma patients are sitting up and talking about going home."

"I'm not just talking about it, doc." She eyed the I.V. again in distaste. "How soon can I get this thing taken out?"

He chuckled. "You're awake. Your vitals are normal. How does now sound?" He mashed the call button on her bed to summon her nurse.

"Not soon enough," she shot back.

He chuckled as he pressed his stethoscope to her chest and listened. "You've got a steady triple beat going. I think it's saying, *Send me home! Send me home!*"

"Cute." She rolled her eyes at him, just glad that he wasn't arguing about keeping her another night.

Of course, Brody had to get all overprotective again and cross-examine the doctor about how to properly care for a concussed patient.

"Minimum two weeks of rest," the doctor informed Brody flatly, not even looking at her. "I raised a few cowgirls, myself, so I understand how difficult a set of marching orders it's going to be. That means no jumping, no running, no four-wheeling, no off-roading, no horseback riding, no—"

"We get it!" Bree snapped. "Two weeks of knitting and cross-stitching it is." *Over my dead body!* There was no reason she couldn't still cook for the ranch hands and maintain most of her normal routines.

"One of us does, anyway." Brody snickered. "Fortunately, this ol' farm boy knows a thing or two about hog tying."

As Bree looked around for something to throw at him, he rolled the water cart safely out of her reach. She had to settle for sticking her tongue out at him.

"Real mature," he mouthed behind the doctor's back.

Within the hour, she was showered and changed into a fresh shirt and pair of jeans that her brother had tossed into an overnight bag. It was too bad he'd forgotten about including her makeup kit. *Guys!* She supposed she should be glad he remembered her under-things.

The only downside of getting out of bed for the first time in three days was how incredibly stiff and sore she felt with each step. Plus, she was so unsteady on her feet that she was half tempted to steal Brody's cane. Then there was the blasted ache in the back of her skull.

"This is what is must feel like to get hit by a train," she muttered to herself as she hobbled her way out of the bathroom and back into the suffocatingly small hospital room. Golly, but she was beyond ready to return home to their wide open fields, farm fresh air, and canyon views!

"May as well have been a train," a sympathetic voice answered. "I heard it was a dump truck that took a swipe at you."

She glanced up to see a nurse assistant waiting for

her with a wheelchair in the doorway. *Oh, yay! I get to scoot my way out of here like an old granny.*

Not in the mood to chit-chat about the accident, she muttered, "Thanks for the ride." Hobbling her way across the room, she sat with a short huff of pain. Man, but even the simplest movements hurt, like sitting and holding her overnight bag on her lap. It was going to be a fun next few days...not.

Brody limped alongside her wheelchair as they made their way to the front entrance of the hospital. "Everyone is looking forward to having you back home where you belong." They passed through a double set of doors leading from the patient ward to the main hallway of the hospital. Passing the elevators, they arrived at the sunny, glassed-in atrium. Straight ahead was the revolving door that would take them outside.

No doubt. His words made her smile. Folks always missed the cook. Then a thought struck her. "About my truck?" She shot Brody a questioning look, wondering what had become of it.

He shook his head sadly. "Totaled, I'm afraid. I'm dealing with the insurance company to get it replaced."

"One less truck to drive home this afternoon, huh?" She didn't even want to think about what the collision was going to do to their insurance premiums.

"Actually, there's still two."

What? She scowled in confusion.

"Yep. Matt's been driving back and forth every day to check on us, deliver supplies, and keep me informed about ranch business. He's out front, waiting for us now."

She bit her lower lip, not liking the reminder that they had a new manager on the payroll. "I thought you had Harley for stuff like that."

Brody snorted. "Harley has more than enough on his plate herding cattle. Told me at least a dozen times already how glad he is to have Matt's help with all the administrative stuff."

The nursing assistant rolled her inside the first section of the revolving door, momentarily separating her from Brody. In seconds, he rejoined them on the other side.

She made a face at him as they paused by the curb. "Maybe the two of you should write a song about this Matt Romero," she noted dryly. "All you've done is sing the man's praises ever since I woke up."

"Thanks, I think." There was no mistaking the Texas drawl that washed over them. It was a nice voice, despite Bree's determination not to like the owner of it. Low and husky with a hint of challenge.

Setting her teeth together, she slowly raised her head to meet the curious gaze of their new ranch manager. Though Brody had warned her, she experienced a jolt at how much he resembled the one man in the world she'd hoped to high heaven she'd never have to lay eyes on again. He wasn't just good looking in his black t-shirt and distressed jeans; he was downright lethal. Just like Cory had been.

She steeled her heart. *Give me an ugly, honest guy any day over the likes of you!* "You must be Matt Romero." She sounded so sullen and resentful that Brody rolled his eyes at her as he moved to assist her from the wheelchair.

"Play nice," he muttered in her ear as he eased her to her feet.

To her dismay, he gently spun her around to face Matt and gave her a nudge. She swayed toward all five feet ten inches of his solidly stacked frame. *Jeez Louise!* She'd never met an Army Ranger before, but it made her wonder if they all tended to be the musclebound, Terminator type. No doubt every female in a fifty-mile radius would be sighing and swooning over him before long.

"Nice to meet you, Bree." His dark gaze swept her face and registered sympathy.

I look that bad, huh? She raised her chin and leaned on him as little as possible while he assisted her into a white truck she didn't recognize.

Scowling over Matt's shoulder at her brother, she was furious to note his casual wave and triumphant smile.

Oh, you are so not leaving me alone with this guy!

"Figured you two could use some getting-to-know-you time," he announced airily, as if her eyes weren't shooting bullet holes straight through his faded plaid shirt.

That's it, she inwardly vowed. *I'm going to burn your eggs and bacon for the rest of the year. No, for the rest of the century!*

With one last wave, her brother disappeared from view.

Matt slid behind the wheel and revved the motor. "Is the A/C on the right temperature for you?"

"It's fine," she muttered, refusing to look at him. Then she gave lie to her words by giving a violent shiver that made her head ache. *Ow!*

"Liar," Matt said softly and reached over to turn up the thermostat.

"I heard Emmitt McCarty gave you a speeding ticket." It was highly uncharitable of her to start off on such a negative topic, but she wasn't in the mood to play nice. *Sorry, not sorry, Brody! Your fault for leaving me alone with the big, bad wolf.* She wasn't buying his story that "he'd picked the right guy this time around." More than likely, Matt Romero was just another opportunist taking advantage of her crippled, too-nice-for-his-own-good brother. Give it a little time, and she would happily deliver Brody a big, fat I-told-you-so.

Matt gave a rumbly chuckle. "He started to, but things got a little too hectic out there on the highway for him to finish the deed."

So you broke the law and got away with it. Lucky you. "Brody is really grateful you decided to speed that day. He says you saved my life." Her words still sounded less than charitable. However, if he was expecting her to kiss his feet after hoodwinking her brother into hiring him, he was in for a big surprise. She lifted her chin, trying to look severe, but ruined the effect by shivering again.

"You still cold?" Muttering something under his breath, Matt turned up his thermostat a second time.

"I'm always cold." She glanced out the window. "Put the temp wherever you want it. I don't expect you to boil on my behalf."

To her irritation, he didn't answer, which was way too bad. She was in the mood to argue.

As the silence between them dragged on, a new idea struck her. Every thirty seconds or so, she forced another shiver, wondering how many times he'd be dumb enough to keep turning up the thermostat. The answer was several more times, as it turned out.

She had to muffle a laugh when a bead of sweat formed on his forehead.

"Hey, ah..." He didn't break the silence until he turned onto the final highway leading to the Anderson ranch. Though it boasted two lanes, it was little more than a paved cow path — winding, poorly banked in places, and no shoulder. "I can only imagine what you're feeling over there. Brody explained why it might be hard for you to look at me for the next few days."

Only the next few days? Try forever! She gritted her teeth, not wanting to discuss anything remotely connected to Cody Satan Brooks. The long driveway entrance to home popped into view. Bree's gaze landed on the big iron A set inside a star over the entry post, and she nearly cried in relief.

We're home!

"I'm not him, Bree, and I'm going to do everything in my power to prove it to you."

What? You're still talking? A sideways glance at Matt Romero showed a trickle of sweat running down his temple and disappearing in his beard.

"Good," she said softly, not daring to risk more than a single syllable. She was too close to laughing.

"Okay, then," he sighed, as if relieved to hear something affirmative from her. He drove her all the way to the front porch where her and Brody's two Old English Sheep dogs were lounging.

Tramp and Lady perked their ears and shot to their feet, tails wagging. Matt leaped down from the driver's seat and hurried around to open the door for her.

Without thinking, she waved a hand in front of her face, wildly grateful for the light breeze whipping its way across the Texas panhandle today.

Matt's dark gaze narrowed on her face. "Are you hot?"

"Gosh, yes!" She fanned her face again for good measure before reluctantly placing her hands on his hard, bunched shoulders. "It's hot as blazes in here."

"Wish you'd have said something." He sounded so exasperated that her heart sang with glee. "I honestly thought you were cold."

"Whatever gave you that idea?" She treated him

to her most innocent look as he lifted her to the ground like she weighed next to nothing.

His upper lip curled sardonically, as the realization sank home that he'd been played. "You're a hard woman, Bree Anderson," he sighed.

And don't you forget it. She blasted him with the full frost of her gaze. "It was nice chatting."

CHAPTER 4: NEW MANAGEMENT

Matt

Matt was too dazed to immediately step away. Like a complete idiot, he remained standing there with his hands on Bree's tiny waist, trying to make sense out of what had just happened.

Her impossibly blue eyes stared back defiantly, making him want to groan out loud. They'd gotten off on the wrong foot, though — for the life of him — he couldn't fathom how he could have avoided it. The fact that she didn't like the way he looked wasn't going to be an easy hurdle to cross. Never before had a woman gazed at him with such blind and rabid contempt. It was both disconcerting and irritating, since he knew he'd done nothing to deserve it.

Equally disconcerting and irritating was the fact that he was attracted to her, which made no sense whatsoever. She totally wasn't his type. She was too thin, too pale, had on zero makeup, and was making every effort to rouse his dislike. *Shoot!* She wasn't even nice. Not even a little. In fact, he couldn't recall ever meeting anyone ruder. Which he found oddly and inexplicably refreshing.

As far as he could tell, she hadn't once ogled his pecs or his biceps. If anything, she seemed to be trying to avoid looking at him, altogether. Which made him want to work all that much harder to be the kind of guy she wouldn't mind looking at. Eventually. After she forgave him for having the misfortune to resemble the one guy in the world she despised the most.

He was tired of dealing with the kind of women who went nutso over a guy, just because of his looks. Or his military uniform. Or the fact he'd trained for and participated in so many extreme physical challenges that he possessed the physique of a bodybuilder. Well, no one was going to accuse Bree Anderson of going ga-ga over him.

"Are you trying to decide if you should have left me in my truck?" she inquired coolly, glancing pointedly down at his hands.

"Nah." Lips twitching at her never-ending sass, he hastily dropped his arms and scrambled for a clever comeback. "Just trying to give you enough time to find all the proof you need."

"Proof?" She arched her brows at him.

"That I'm not the jerk who hurt you."

She sucked in a breath. "I'm well aware you're not

him." Her smile didn't reach her eyes. "For one thing, he considered himself way too cool to ever break a sweat. For another thing, he wore too much hairspray to pull off the whole wind-blown thing you've got going on." She wiggled her fingers expressively in the air.

"Yeah, well, cool isn't generally what I strive to be," he assured dryly, liking the fact that she didn't seem too turned off by the sight of a guy sweating.

"Oh? What is it that you strive to be, Matt Romero?" she shot back. Her blue gaze sharpened despite the weary lines beneath her eyes.

"Successful in everything I do," he returned evenly. "And right now that entails securing a patent for your brother's latest horticultural break-through."

She made a face. "Do you have any idea what a patent costs?"

"I know what his is costing us. Eleven thousand, four hundred, seventy-three dollars, and twenty-six cents, including the attorney fees for drafting it."

"That's an oddly specific number."

"No kidding. Gotta love dealing with the government." He dug for the receipt in his back pocket, unfolded it, and held it up for her to see. It was stamped with today's date, since he'd only made the online payment a few hours ago.

She snatched the slip of paper from him. "You actually filed for Brody's patent," she breathed. "How? Did you rob a bank?"

"Nothing that exciting, Miss Anderson. All I did was sell some mutual fund shares."

She nodded sagely as she returned the receipt to him. "It was a very generous but very foolish thing to do." She still wasn't smiling, and there was still zero approval in her body language.

Oka-a-a-ay. "Thank you for calling me generous. Not overly thrilled about being called a fool." He waited for her to explain. Man, but she was turning out to be a hard nut to crack!

"You'll find out soon enough for yourself." Her voice was bitter. "No one is ever going to pay what our beef is worth. I should know. I've tried peddling it to every major restaurant and grocery store in a hundred-mile radius. Though my memories are a little hazy on the topic, Brody swears that's what I was doing the day I got caught in that highway pileup."

For a moment, the brittleness in her eased, and Matt was struck by the raw vulnerability he read in her features. Apparently, the car accident had her a lot more rattled than she was letting on. Knowing she wouldn't appreciate having any attention drawn to that fact, he hastened to ask, "Did any of these restaurants and grocery stores give you a reason for turning you down?" He folded him arms, studying the fascinating array of expressions flitting across her classically oval features.

"They sure did, though I didn't have the heart to

break it to Brody." She muffled a yawn, looking more tired than ever.

"Then break it to me." Maybe it was wrong of him to detain a woman practically teetering on her feet from a concussion, but he urgently needed the kind of insight only she could provide if he was going to do his job.

"If you insist, Mr. Ranch Manager," she retorted sarcastically. "It's pretty simple. No matter how good our beef tastes, folks aren't going to pay the price of a twelve or fourteen-ounce steak for a double-patty burger."

The price of a steak, eh? Based on the first few sets of numbers he'd run, Bree's analogy sounded pretty accurate. "Then maybe we need to come up with a new marketing strategy." He idly ran a hand over his chin. "Or a whole new production plan."

"Like what?" she demanded irritably.

"I don't know, Bree," he sighed. "Still working on that." *I just arrived into town, remember?*

"Impressive," she muttered beneath her breath and started to push past him.

Her disdain was starting to wear on him. "You seem to know an awful lot about what your customers don't want," he noted coolly. "I'd kinda like to focus what they do want and deliver that, alright?"

Her steps slowed. "If you think for one second Brody and I haven't worked our fingers to the bone doing exactly that," she gritted out, "then you're out of your mind!"

Great! Now my sanity is up for question. "Or, here's a thought," he retorted. "We could stop trading insults long enough to have a serious conversation."

"About what?" she snapped.

"About whatever scenarios would make your customers shell out the kind of dough Anderson beef is actually worth."

She whirled dizzily to face him once more. "They'd only pay those kinds of prices at five star dining establishments. We're talking filet mignon, ribeye, top sirloin, porterhouse, and New York strip steak. Not burgers and fries in the middle of podunk Texas. We're sorta dead in the water here, Matt, in case you haven't noticed."

Now we're getting somewhere! He liked that he'd hit a nerve, that he'd finally gotten her to show a little passion about something. Maybe they'd never be friends, but this was the kind of communicating it was going to take to work together. "Then maybe we should open one of those five-star dining establishments."

"In podunk Texas, huh? I guess you missed that part." With a withering look, she continued her slow, hitching promenade to the front porch.

"Aren't you enrolled in some culinary program?" he called after her. His brain was already cranking out a whole new set of possibilities. Bree Anderson might be about as friendly as a rattlesnake, but it sounded as if she knew just about everything there was to know about steak. He could certainly use that to their advantage.

"Can't hear you." She waved a hand dismissively. "Too far away."

He watched as she attempted to sail away from him with her head held high, though her pained gait made it impossible to pull it off with any grace. He didn't dare offer her any assistance with the porch stairs, for fear of getting his head bitten off, though he feared she might have trouble making it up all ten of them.

She paused at the base of the stairs. Any onlooker would've assumed she'd stopped merely to pet the sheep dogs, but he knew better. She needed to rest a moment before starting her ascent. She was a much weaker version of herself than before the accident. Anyone in her shoes would've been. She'd taken a pretty good bump to the head.

Moving silently closer, in the event she required his assistance — unwanted or not — he surveyed the Anderson's massive ranch home with no small amount of interest. It was perched on an incline, which lent the stucco two-and-a-half story structure a towering effect. Symmetrical additions had been constructed on both the east and the west side, and it was capped with brick-red roof tiles that were as decorative as they were practical. Of all the choices of materials on the market, the composite tiles stood the best chance of withstanding the heavy wind and hail that so often plagued the region.

Matt felt Bree watching him out of the corner of her eye, though she was pretending he wasn't there. He took a step in her direction, then another one, wondering if she was inwardly hoping he would offer to help her. She was way too proud to ask, of course.

In the split second between when he hesitated to speak and when she laid her hand on the porch railing, a man on horseback ambled up the gravel drive. He clip-clopped their way from the direction of the big, red barn behind the house. Matt glanced up to find Harley's grizzled features stretched into a smile as bright as a thousand candles. He wasn't looking at Matt, though. He only had eyes for Bree as he hopped down from his horse, a palomino mare the color of butterscotch, and angled his head at Matt to take the reins.

Matt wordlessly complied, grateful not to have to watch Bree trip or collapse out of sheer stubbornness of trying to prove she didn't need his help. She sagged all too quickly against Harley's side, allowing him to guide her all the way through the front door. His slightly bowed legs were covered in chaps, and his spurs jingled with each step.

"I missed home," Matt overheard her murmur against the older fellow's shoulder before the screen door bounced shut behind them. Unless it was the wind whistling in his ears, there was a tremor in her voice.

"We missed you, too, sweet girl, every last one of

us," Harley returned fervently before their voices faded.

Sweet girl! Sweet girl? Matt stared after them in amazement. Boy, did she have Harley fooled!

Brody, who had followed Matt's truck up the gravel driveway and circled behind the house to park the horse trailer, hobbled around the corner of the porch. He dug his cane with energy into the gravel.

Taking one look at Matt's sweaty face, he burst out laughing. "Looks like your first encounter with Bree was pretty memorable."

Matt shrugged. "It was alright." Though she'd been prickly and difficult, she'd helped shed some light on a few really important issues.

"Is that why you're sweating?"

Matt shrugged. "It's hot out." Yeah, Bree's antics with the thermostat in his truck cab probably had more to do with his sweat than the dry summer heat. However, nothing good would come of ratting her out to her brother. If he was going to earn her trust, he was going to have to be patient. He already had a few ideas to try out during their next encounter.

Brody scanned his features, then sighed. "Mind joining me in the office? We might as well jump right into ranch business."

"Not at all." Matt had been hoping Brody could spare the time to go over his initial assessment of the books. He pointed at the side entrance to the sunroom that the Anderson's had converted into their home office. "Harley's helping Bree get situated inside. As soon as he gets back, I can join you." He nodded at the horse, whose reins he was still holding.

For an answer, Brody put two fingers to his mouth and gave a sharp whistle. One of the stable hands came skidding around the corner, all geared up in chaps and spurs like Harley.

"Yeah, boss?"

If Matt's memory served, the cowboy's name was Crew. According to Harley, who had briefed him on their personnel, Crew was a high school drop out. One whose eyes were nearly the same shade of sapphire as the Andersons. What was with all these blue-eyed Texans between Hereford and Amarillo? Was it something in the water? Though Bree and Brody were only related to their parents by adoption, they could've passed for biological relations because of their eyes, alone.

The resemblance stopped there, though. Where Brody's face exuded a weary sort of wisdom, Crew's was plain devilish. That said, the twenty-two-year-old had a reputation for working hard and seemed to know a lot about herding cattle. Harley was currently training him as a backup range rider. And when the tall, wiry cowboy wasn't out herding or riding, he stayed busy doing whatever else Harley assigned him — everything from filling troughs, to raking hay, to repairing fences, to mucking stalls.

Brody pointed at Harley's palomino. "I need you to take Penny off our hands. Not sure if Harley plans to ride her some more today or what."

Crew smirked at Matt. "We'll be back on patrol in about an hour. Right now, Harley has Nash and Zane out rotating the herd to the east pasture."

By now, Matt was starting to understand that the frequent rotation of the Anderson herd around the ranch was part of Brody's special diet for their cattle. The animals were on a pretty strict regimen that involved timed grazing patterns in specific fields — corn, wheat, and alfalfa. A setup that impressed Matt as every shade of genius. He was more convinced than ever that he'd accidentally gotten in on the ground floor of something really special in the making. All the Andersons really needed was someone to help them market and package their brand. Someone like him.

"All sounds good, Crew." Brody glanced at his watch. "I'll let Harley know you've got his horse if I run into him."

"Roger that, boss."

Brody motioned for Matt to follow him inside.

Matt watched Crew's retreat before stepping after Brody, unsure of what his smirk was all about. He really hoped he was wrong about the guy, but Crew had been giving him bad vibes since day one. It was as if he had something to hide. It was also pretty clear he didn't like Matt, though he seemed to be making an effort to keep that fact from both Harley and Brody. Then again, Matt was still sizing up the guy and taking mental notes. He wasn't interested in getting into a spitting match with someone who might merely require more time to adjust to a change in management. For some folks, change could be a bumpy process.

Since the Anderson's business office had once been used as a sunroom, it was long and narrow. There was a wall of windows on one side and a wall of cabinets and drawers on the other. Three desks were rowed up end-to-end in the center, leaving only the narrowest of walkways on both sides. Brody had made it clear to Matt he could claim the one at the far end of the room, which he'd done. He suspected it was once used by the hated Cory Brooks. Regardless, he'd spent the last three days cleaning out drawers and making it his.

At the center desk sat Bree, not even attempting to rest. She was hunched over a computer with Harley leaning over her shoulder. Both were frowning at her screen.

"Is this your idea of R&R?" Brody teased, drumming his knuckles on his own desk as he moved behind it to boot up his laptop.

She made a face without looking up. "Hey, the doc said no cartwheels, jet skiing, or skydiving. I don't recall him saying anything against sitting on my bum and using my eyeballs."

He ignored her fussing. "How's that noggin of yours feeling?"

Instead of answering, she pointed at the screen. "I think you need to take a look at this."

Though not invited, Matt moved farther into the

room to join their huddle. It appeared they were staring at an Excel spreadsheet, but the numbers were too tiny for him to read from where he stood. "What are we looking at?" He bent closer, curious at what had Bree so worked up. He was secretly glad it had nothing to do with him this time around.

"Inventories," she supplied grimly. "Dwindling ones. I noticed some minor discrepancies about a year ago, but they were so small that I initially chalked them up to clerical errors. A missing roll of hay here and a few bags of feed there. But ever since then, I've been religiously tracking them. Actually going out to the barn lofts and hand counting stuff, in some instances." She shook her head in disgust. "I really hate to break it to you, but I think a clear pattern is emerging. One that suggests we have an employee skimming the supplies."

"And the calves," Harley growled. He shoved his dusty Stetson farther back on his head. "See here." He stabbed a finger at Bree's computer screen. "A year ago, we wrote off calf 5620 for miscellaneous reasons. This year, we never recorded the tag for 5621 as having ever been used. We went from calf 5521 and skipped straight to calf 5721."

"How many calves are missing, altogether?" Matt asked. His mind was already churning its way through the possibilities.

"Only two, if these numbers are correct."

"Only two!" Brody fumed. "That's eight hundred pounds of beef, I'll have you know."

"And the bales of hay?" Matt pressed. He might not be an experienced rancher, but he was highly skilled at running Army operations. And he was particularly good at debugging processes and figuring out how to make things work more efficiently. In this particular instance, his gut was telling him they were looking at more than a bit of cattle rustling. Yeah, eight hundred pounds of meat was a lot for the average household, but it amounted to beans in the grand scheme of things — definitely not the sign of a major castle rustling ring at work.

"About one per month after the first calf was written off for miscellaneous reasons. It went up to two per month around the time we skipped recording calf 5621."

"So someone stole two of our calves, and now they're skimming the supplies they need to raise them." Twin spots of red formed on Brody's cheeks.

"But why?" Harley rocked back on his heels, hooking his thumbs in the belt loops of his jeans. "A full-grown calf is ready for slaughter by Day 367 or thereabouts. By my calculations, the first calf that went missing would be well past that age, sitting at 396 days or more."

Matt frowned in concentration, still assessing the pieces of the puzzle and trying to fit them together. "What else is missing?"

Bree clasped her hands so tightly that her knuckles turned white. She looked so stressed that he could only presume she was blaming herself to an extent. "Vitamins. Corn feed. That special hybrid alfalfa you've been tinkering with, Brody. Plus a few jars of the molasses we pour on the corn silage for the calves."

"Again, why?" Harley groused. "Why keep fattening 'em up past the standard slaughter age?"

Matt and Brody exchanged a heavily charged look, after which Brody pulled over the nearest office chair and took a seat in horrified silence.

"What?" Bree cried, looking more alarmed than ever as she glanced between her brother and Matt. "What are you not telling me?"

When Brody continued to stare blindly out the sunroom windows, Matt declared, "Reverse engineering would be my guess. Someone is trying to back their way into your brother's patent formula."

"My life work," Brody chimed in dully. "Hundreds of hours of research. Possibly thousands, and someone is trying to steal it."

"Who would do such a thing?" Bree gasped. "I mean, I trust the guys. They're loyal and hardworking, and every one of them has been with us for years. Why, even Crew just passed the one-year mark." Her voice dwindled as her gaze fell on Matt and hardened.

"Don't, Bree." Brody's voice was bleak. "Don't even look at him like that."

"Well, he's our newest employee," she snapped.

"Oh, for crying out loud!" Matt glared back, taking a few steps away from their huddle to hitch his hip on the corner of his desk. "Two years ago I was stationed overseas at...never mind. It's classified. A year ago I was at Ft. Lewis. Two months ago, I out-processed at Ft. Benning. And, no." He folded his arms in defiance. "There's no place to keep a spare cow in a guy's barracks room, trust me. Much less two cows."

She snickered without humor. "What I'm hearing is a whole lot of protesting from someone who claims he's innocent."

"He *is* innocent, and you know it." Brody twisted a piece of paper off the corner of a document resting in front of him, wadded it, and tossed it in her direction. "The guy just invested more than eleven grand of his own funds in my patent."

She batted it away. "Or," she countered testily, "he invested eleven grand to get you to share it with him."

"Nice try, but he never saw the formula." Brody tossed another wad of paper at her. "I handed it directly to our attorney. Matt wasn't in the room at the time."

Harley made an impatient sound. "Well, look at the time, folks." He wrinkled his nose at the clock on the wall. "I'm due to be back on the range soon, so I'll skedaddle." He shot a half-amused, half-sympathetic look in Matt's direction. "Do me a favor and get all the ravaging of my good name out of the way while I'm gone."

"As if anyone would suspect you," Bree scoffed.

The look she tossed over her shoulder at him was undeniably affectionate.

He waved a finger teasingly at her. "Maybe that's my angle. The guy you'd least suspect." He dropped his voice to a low and menacing note on the last word.

"Oh, come on!" She pushed his hand away. "You share a cottage with three other workers. Can't think of any place you'd hide a pair of calves in there."

He pretended to consider her words for a moment. "Might not hurt to check the pantry, just to be on the safe side. Or the storm cellar, come to think of it."

"And his sock drawer," Brody added dryly. "He's got pretty big feet."

"See what I have to put up with around here?" Harley's features registered mock outrage. "No respect."

Though Matt spared him a tight smile, his gut told him that Harley was only trying to lighten the mood in the room. No one had truly considered him a suspect, not even for a second. Bree, on the other hand, was still glowering at Matt.

Brody waited until Harley made his exit before continuing his tirade. "I know you've been otherwise occupied the last few days, Bree, so your confusion on the matter is understandable. But know this." His jaw tightened. "Our attorney drafted a contract that makes Matt a partner in both the profits and the losses of our ranch. If we fail, he stands to lose a hundred percent of his investment. He truly has no incentive to do anything but strive for success."

When Brody paused in sober contemplation, Matt picked up the thread of conversation and carried it a step further. "So what's at stake for you, Bree?"

She sucked in a breath of sheer outrage. "How *dare* you! This is my home."

"Whoa! Time out, you two." Brody came out of his chair, slapping one hand against the other to form a T.

"No, I'd kinda like a shot at answering his question," she snarled.

"Just stop," her brother pleaded. "No one in this room is a suspect. The three of us are on the same team, and we better start acting like it." He leaned heavily on the desk in front of him. "If we don't, we're not going to stand a chance at routing out the real saboteur."

"A team, huh?" Bree ducked back behind her computer screen. "Funny I don't recall being consulted about the latest addition to our so-called team."

"He saved your life, Bree, and he's doing everything in his power to help save our ranch."

"Why?" The full force of her glare returned to Matt. "Why did you do it?"

"Save your life?" He wasn't sure which question to answer first. "Because I'm a soldier, I guess. It's what we're trained to do. Defend and protect. It didn't matter who you were. Male or female, young or old. I would've dived into that truck after anyone."

"And our ranch." She watched him closely. "Why did you decide to come work for us?"

That was an even easier answer to give. "I needed a job."

"You could've gotten a job anywhere."

True. If it weren't for that vehicle pileup on the interstate, he'd probably be employed at Pantex by now. "Yeah, well, I happened to have Brody Anderson filling my ears with stuff about faith and fate."

"So you believe in fairytales, huh?"

He gave a short laugh. "Let's just say I believe in Brody and leave it at that."

"Appreciate it," Brody interjected dryly. "Now that we've taken another round of pot shots at each other, can we wave the white flag and move on to the next line of business?" He shuffled around a few stacks of paper on his desk. "Like how we're going to catch ourselves a saboteur?"

"Sure." Bree's voice was deceptively sweet. "We can do that right after Matt fills you in on his latest brainstorm about transforming one of our barns into a high-end steakhouse."

"Do what?" Her brother's jaw dropped.

"Build a five-star restaurant right here on the ranch." She propped her elbows on her desk to rest her chin on her hands. She adopted a faux dreamy look. "But why stop there? We could add loft suites and balconies with hot tubs and upgrade it to a flipping B&B, while we're at it. I'm talking honeymoon packages complete with trail rides, canyon tours, and..." Her voice faded beneath Matt's admiring grin. "Now, what?" she muttered sarcastically, shifting self-consciously in her seat.

You're so beautiful when you're mad. So fiercely passionate and alive. He was completely wowed out by her brilliance and energy level, especially considering how recently she'd vacated her hospital bed. There was depth to her — real depth — even if she was a bit difficult to get along with. What was more, she was also starting to appeal to him on levels he didn't want to dissect too closely. Pale and skinny cowgirls had never been his thing. It must be the heat getting to him.

To cover his confusion, he fell back on the old tried-and-true needling method. She sorta had it coming, anyway. "Gee, Brody!" he teased. "Does your sister always do her best thinking when she's all worked into a lather?" Without waiting for an answer, he glanced around the room in search of something red. "Because if that's the case, we could keep a matador cape on hand and come up with some sort of run-with-the-bulls routine for her to help us keep our business meetings productive."

Her brother waved a hand to brush aside his jibe. "All bull horns aside, can we circle back to the B&B idea? Because we might actually be on to something there."

I know, right? Matt liked how quick Brody was to

pick up on the possibilities. It reaffirmed his own belief that the answer to their financial problems might already be staring them in the face.

"You've got to be kidding me!" Bree exploded, head moving back and forth between them. "I was joking. For reals." She gave Matt a particularly hard look. "Then again, maybe I'm still in a coma. Or Alice in Wonderland on round two in the rabbit hole." She pushed to her feet with a wince that made Matt tense to spring, should his assistance be required. "Either way, I can tell I'm outnumbered now that you two are in cahoots with each other. For this reason, I'm going to blow this taco stand. You can chuckle all you want behind my back."

As she spun away from her desk, she stumbled.

Matt was there, hands moving beneath her elbows to steady her.

"This is just a bad dream, isn't it?" she muttered. "I'm going to close my eyes, and you'll disappear."

It was like holding a snarling tiger, but something deep and elemental wrenched inside Matt's chest. He didn't know what it was about this particular woman, only that never before had he felt so protective of another human being. The longing to cuddle her closer slammed in to him, though he resisted it, along with the need to prove to her that he was someone she could trust. Not all men his approximate height and build were bad. Someday he'd make her see that. Then maybe, just maybe, she'd open those incredible eyes of hers and they'd be spitting something besides blue flames in his direction.

As he met her brother's half-curious, half-concerned look above his sister's head, Matt's thoughts underwent another metamorphosis. Then again, maybe a fellow could get used to blue fire. Maybe the spark and heat of it was just who Bree Anderson was. Maybe he didn't want to change a thing about her, after all.

CHAPTER 5: A BROTHER'S FAITH

Bree

Bree had to hold herself stiff to keep from closing the short distance between them and melting into Matt's embrace. She didn't want him to keep playing the part of her gentle savior, didn't want his sympathy or his kindness, because it was making it all that much harder to hate him. She didn't want him on their ranch or in their lives.

It didn't help that she knew she was being unfair, unreasonable, and everything else in between. She seriously just couldn't bear to look at the guy. Why, oh, why did Brody have to go and hire someone who so closely resembled her ex? It really wasn't fair.

Matt's voice was low and husky in her ear. "Would it help if I wore a mask?"

No doubt he was trying to be funny but, for some reason, it made her want to weep. Without answering, she wrenched away from his gentle grasp and left the office. She barely made it past the doorway before tears burned behind her eyelids and slid weakly down her face. Fortunately, her room was on the first level of the ranch, so she didn't have to fight her way up the stairs, a detail that only served to make her silent sobs come harder.

The master bedroom suite shouldn't have been occupied by her. It should've still held the kindhearted Andersons. But between old-age and cancer, among other health complications, both of her adoptive parents had passed three years ago, leaving her and Brody to fend for themselves.

She thought she heard quiet steps behind her, but she didn't turn around to see who it was. Reaching her bedroom, she let herself inside. Then she headed straight for her four-poster bed and eased herself atop the mattress. Her adoptive mother, Shanna Anderson, had sewn the cotton eyelet pillowcase by hand, lovingly embroidering each pale blue rosette along the edge of it. Her handiwork was everywhere in the house, in every room and on every stick of furniture. It was an ever-present reminder of how much she'd loved her family and how hard she'd worked to transform these adobe walls into a home.

To this day, Bree didn't understand what had made Mom and Pops Anderson decide to adopt two teens from foster care. Her adoptive father's name was Oran, but everyone had just called him Pops. They were older at the time, both in their early seventies. Some said it was their age, that they were hoping for a little extra help around the ranch — the built-in kind. But Bree knew better. The truth was, they could've hired more help if help was all they'd wanted.

For some reason, Mom and Pops had decided in their twilight years that they wanted the family they'd never had, the children Mom had never been able to bear. And Bree and Brody had been the huge benefactors of their longing to parent, to mentor, and to nurture.

Just thinking of their infinite capacity for love made Bree finish dissolving. *Why?* She wanted to wail her heartache to the ceiling. *Why did you have to leave us so soon? We weren't near finished needing you.*

In the three short years they'd been gone, Bree and Brody had bungled just about everything there was to bungle on the ranch. Neither of them possessed very strong business skills. That was why it had been so easy for Cory Brooks to sweep into their lives and take advantage of them. Brody was a farmer and a dreamer, an overly trusting one at that. Bree was the opposite when it came to trusting people, but she'd proven equally unskilled at ranching. She seriously just wanted to cook, bake, and feed people.

Turning her face into her pillow, she wept until she could barely continue breathing through her nose. Then she reached for the box of tissues on her nightstand and whimpered her way through a small mountain of tissues. Blowing her nose made her head hurt, but apparently that was the cost of breathing today. At some point, she must have cried herself to sleep.

She woke for tiny patches of time throughout the afternoon, and each time Brody was there. He took her temperature and made her sit up and sip on various beverages, everything from green tea to chicken broth. But each time, she couldn't wait to close her eyes again.

"It's good to have you home again," he whispered each time before leaving the room.

She knew she should be doing something besides lying around in bed, as useless as a slug, but she couldn't seem to find the strength to get up.

Though Bree forced herself to dress and leave her room for short periods of time over the next several days, it took the better part of two weeks before she was feeling even remotely like her old self again.

Most unfortunately, feeling like her old self didn't erase the fact that Brody had hired a new ranch manager. In the past, she'd enjoyed starting her mornings with a mug of coffee on the east side of the veranda, soaking up the first rays of morning. However, Matt Romero was living in Pops' hunting cabin these days. That meant he was halfway up the ridge that formed Sidewinder Canyon on the outer forty acres.

Though the cottonwood trees and chokeberry

bushes were in full bloom this time of year, filling in the mesquites and red cedars to form a lush barrier between here and there, Bree still felt that Matt's presence on their property was encroaching upon her privacy. And her breathing room. And he most definitely was messing with her peace of mind.

Try as she might, she still had a difficult time being in the same room with him. The memories he evoked were too acute, too painful. Yeah, he had some good ideas about improvements they could and should be making to the ranch. And sure, he seemed to be building a decent rapport with the ranch hands quicker than she expected. And sure, the day-to-day operations of farming and herding seemed to be running more smoothly beneath his management. But that didn't make it any easier for her to look at him.

Unable to completely give up her morning ritual of watching the sun rise, Bree opted to carry her coffee to the screened-in porch out back. She settled on the porch swing, pushing it into motion with her toe and turning her face toward the east. She wouldn't get the first shoots of light from here, but she'd get the glow and the warmth.

"There you are." The same darkly handsome cowboy, who seemed to be occupying way too much of her head space lately, strode up the back stairs two at a time to join her on the back porch. "Been looking all over for you, chef." He had a manila folder in hand, resting against his thigh.

"I wasn't hiding." Nudging the floor a little harder with the toe of her boot, she rocked more vigorously on the porch swing while allowing herself a brief glance at him over the top of her coffee mug. Then she returned her gaze to the grazing cattle in the distant pasture.

However, the peek was long enough to note that he was wearing another one of his favorite solid colored t-shirts. Unlike the other employees, he didn't seem to be into plaid shirts and Stetsons. It was plain old jeans and t-shirts for him. A white v-neck, this time, which was completely ridiculous attire for ranch life. It was going to be as dark as sin with dust and grime before long.

"Mind if I join you?" He moved in her direction, gesturing at the empty spot beside her on the swing.

She stopped swinging, opting not to put up a fuss. Maybe if she didn't say much, he would say his piece quickly and leave her alone all the sooner.

"I wanted to run these sketches past you."

She heard the rustle of paper in his hands. *Great.* Whatever he wanted today was apparently going to require looking. She moved her head to watch his movements from the corner of her eye, while raising her mug to take another sip of coffee.

At her hesitation, he sighed, "Good grief, Bree! It's been two weeks." He dug in his pocket for something. "I've tried everything I can think of from growing out my beard to wearing sunglasses inside the office, but you leave me no choice. I guess it's going to take more drastic measures for us to be able to work together."

Or you could just quit. It was an uncharitable thought, one that was accompanied by a stab of guilt. Brody really liked the guy. Apparently Matt was well on the way of putting their books in the black by year-end through his unique brand of management.

Matt set his paperwork between them on the swing and proceeded to fiddle with something on his head. "Okay. You can look now. Matt Romero has left the house. Promise."

She glanced over at him and gave an involuntary snicker. He was wearing a black, superhero mask, one that covered the entire upper half of his face. It had black pointy ears, eyeholes, and a nose shield. The only part of him left fully uncovered was his mouth. His very nice mouth with his very firm lips that were currently quirked into a half-smile. Because of the mask, however, it was much harder to tell if he was laughing at her.

"You're crazy," she muttered, trying not to chuckle again.

"Nope. I'm Batman."

She rolled her eyes. "Are you seriously going to wear that thing around the ranch?"

"Maybe. Like Bruce Wayne said, 'it's not who I am underneath, but what I do that defines me'."

"You're still a nut." She couldn't believe he was actually wearing a mask for her. Though she didn't want to approve of anything he did, it was sort of cute, bordering on endearing.

"Among other things, yes. Can we talk barn renovations now?"

She shook her head in bemusement, still befuddled over the fact that he and Brody were actually noodling around her bed-and-breakfast idea. "All I care about is that the kitchen includes a ten-burner gas stove, double ovens, and a sub-zero fridge." If they were going to dream about castles in the clouds, hers was going to have a commercial grade kitchen, worthy of the top cooking channels.

"So you said the last time we talked." He passed a series of sketches over to her. "I'm getting cost comparisons drawn up for the leading brand appliances. In the meantime, I could use your input on the layout for the kitchen cabinetry."

"You mean we're really doing this?" She laid down her mug on the windowsill before accepting the sketches. It blew her mind that they were really going to transfer the big, red barn out back into a B&B with a high-end steak restaurant.

"Looks like. Brody is all for it, and Harley and his crew are more than ready to start swinging hammers. I told 'em we needed to get your approval on the specs, though, before charging full speed ahead."

The "specs" turned out to be a fully computerized architectural plan, complete with floor layouts, electrical configurations, and construction notes. "Where did you get these?" Bree gasped, thumbing through the pages in wonder. She didn't know the first thing about renovation plans, but she imagined this one must have cost a fortune. It was so detailed, and it clearly had been professionally prepared.

"Computer Science degree, remember? Though my focus was programming, I took a few drafting classes on the side for my elective requirements."

"You did this?" She ventured another look at his masked face and found herself choking back a giggle. "You actually drew these?"

"I'm a man of many talents, Bree. I can do more than rock it in a Batman mask."

Thoroughly knocked off balance by his teasing tone, she quickly returned her attention to his sketches. Otherwise, she might have to acknowledge the fact that his insistence on wearing that silly mask of his was doing crazy little things to her heart. It certainly drew attention to his chocolate brown eyes and the curious, searching way he always seemed to be looking at her. Eyes that in no way reminded her of anyone she was trying to forget. He was fun and flirtatious, without crossing any lines, and he'd managed to capture her attention without creating an awkward or uncomfortable moment between them. For some inexplicable reason, the mask was making it really hard to focus on his sketches, though.

Maybe it wasn't just the mask. Maybe it was the way he had his arm slung across the back of the swing while leaning closer to point out a special detail on the kitchen shelving.

"Doors or no doors, Chef Anderson?" He tapped the top half of the cabinetry over the double sink. "Do you want to be able to reach up and grab, or do you want to hide the clutter?"

She closed her eyes for a moment to visualize herself walking through the layout he'd designed. He had really done a great job of utilizing every inch of space and maximizing the storage capacity of the room. "No doors above the cabinetry on either side of the stove, please. No doors on the cabinets above and below the sink, and no doors on the shelving below the prep station in the center of the room. Everywhere else, I'd welcome the option to hide the clutter." It would ensure easy access to quick-grab items like plates, glasses, mixing bowls, and appliances, while allowing her to stow away dry goods, holiday dishes, and spare linens.

"No problem. What about the ovens? Do you want them stacked or side-by-side? Warming drawers above or below?"

They were so busy examining his drawings and debating the options that neither of them heard Brody's approach until he was practically on top of them.

"I'm not even going to ask about the mask." He gave a bark of laughter that had Matt and Bree jolting away from each other.

Somehow during their conversation, their heads had drifted closer. Close enough for her to catch a whiff of his aftershave, something with overtones of mint and sage.

"Hey, don't knock it unless you've tried it," Matt shot back, patting the side of his mask. "I do some of my best thinking in this thing."

"Didn't it arrive on a FedEx truck an hour ago?" Brody scoffed.

"Yep, and I've been doing my best thinking ever since."

Brody shook his head. "I should have stuck to my original plan and not asked." He glanced furtively at Bree before continuing to address Matt. "Guess I could've just beamed up a bat signal instead of hunting you down, but you've got a visitor out front."

"Matt, baby?" a female voice cried anxiously.

Bree glanced up to find a tall, paper-thin creature in a filmy, off-the-shoulder sundress approaching. She was gliding up the sidewalk that circled the house with an exaggerated swing of her hips, transforming the simple walkway into her personal runway.

"Apparently, she decided not to wait out front," Brody muttered beneath his breath.

Matt abruptly stood. "Candy? What are you doing here?"

"Looking for you, baby. Why else would I drive so far in this insufferable heat?" The platinum blonde mounted the porch stairs and pushed open the screen. Parking her perfect figure in the doorway, she waved her perfect manicure at her perfect makeup, while wrinkling her perfect nose in distaste at their surroundings. Apparently, country chic decor wasn't her thing.

"Why were you looking for me," he returned coolly.

"Because we're still engaged, you crazy Ranger," she cooed, gliding the rest of the way to him. She fluttered her ring finger beneath his nose. The enormous princess-cut diamond on it caught the morning sun and glinted like white fire. "I don't know what made you decide to go all Batman this morning, but I'm totally digging the look." With that, she leaned in to plant a kiss on his lips.

And just like that, the silly mask was no longer cute or funny to Bree. She'd seen and heard enough to know that her first impression about Matt Romero hadn't been wrong. He was a miserable player, like Cory Brooks had been, worming his way into their midst and falsely securing their confidence in him. He'd seemed so sincere, too. She'd almost been fooled into believing his act.

Snatching up her coffee mug, she headed for the door leading inside to the great room.

"You never got around to telling me where you want those warming drawers," Matt called after her.

Maybe that's because our little powwow got cut short by the fiancée you failed to mention you had. Since he was talking, Bree could only presume he was no longer in full lip-lock with the woman, not that it was any of her business. "Put 'em wherever you want." She fought to keep her voice bland. "It really doesn't matter."

"Bree, I really need to know what you want before we—"

She shut the door a little harder than necessary, cutting him off in mid-sentence. Though it was petty and juvenile to slam doors, she knew her quick exit from the porch was by far the best option for them all. She had a temper on her, one she fought all too often to control. Mom had taught her to isolate herself and walk it off when it was starting to simmer like this.

Marching straight through the kitchen, she deposited her mug in the sink and kept walking. Hardly paying any attention to where she was going, she strode up the hallway to the main foyer and out the front door.

Harley was standing at the base of the stairs with his horse's reins in hand, conferring with Crew over a chipped porch railing. Beyond the two men was a shiny yellow Corvette with the motor idling and the driver's door propped open. The sight of it brought on a fresh wave of rage, this time so powerful that Bree nearly choked on it.

"May I?" She motioned for Harley to pass her the reins.

"Aren't you supposed to be on a hiatus from riding?" he asked suspiciously.

"It's been two weeks," she said flatly. "I'm fine."

"But your brother said—"

"Now, Harley! Hand them over now!" She'd never pulled rank on the kind old rancher before. Never once had she said or done anything to remind him whose name appeared on the deed of the property they were standing on, but she was beyond reason. All she knew was that she was desperate to be as far away as possible from the miserable yellow Corvette sitting on the front circle driveway, and from the hateful man standing on the back porch with the car's red-carpet-worthy owner.

Harley wordlessly gave up the reins.

Without pausing to thank him or explain where she was going, she leaped astride the butterscotch mare and dug in her heels. "Let's go," she snapped, lifting the reins.

The mare took off across the yard at a steady trot. Bree leaned forward against the creature's neck, muttering, "Get me out of here, please." Hardly able to focus on her surroundings, she rode the mare down the grassy stretch between the driveway and the fence, heading away from home. By the time she reached the main road, her head was aching so badly that she felt like throwing up. With a groan, she brought the horse to a halt and slid dizzily to the ground. Since she wasn't finished being angry or ready to return home, she kept walking in the same direction she'd been riding.

There was no telling how much time passed before she heard the low rumble of a truck engine. It was one she recognized. Brody had arrived to give her the browbeating she deserved.

He pulled far enough past her so she was facing the back doors of the horse trailer. Then he rolled to a stop and hopped down from the driver's seat. Hobbling her way on his cane, he anxiously scanned her features. "Let's get that horse inside the trailer, Bree."

His words were spoken with such quiet concern that she didn't have the heart to put up a fight. She was in no condition to keep going, at any rate. They both knew that. They worked together in silence to load up the horse. Then she allowed him to lead her to the passenger side of the cab.

Instead of letting him hand her up, however, she tipped her forehead against his shoulder and let the tears flow. "I can't do this anymore, Brody."

"I know," he answered gently. His arms came around her. "I know." He rubbed gentle circles in the middle of her back while she wept.

It was a long time before he finished lifting her inside the truck. When he restarted the motor, however, he didn't head back toward the ranch like she expected. He continued on down the two-lane highway, passing up the road leading to town.

And then she knew. He was driving her to the old white church at the base of the canyon. It was Saturday morning, so there were no services scheduled, which meant they were most likely paying a visit to the adjacent cemetery.

"Mom and Pops would be so ashamed of me," she murmured damply.

"Not true." He reached across the cab to take her hand.

"I try so hard. I really do," she moaned. "I cook the recipes she taught me and even bumble my way through an embroidery project now and then. I've kept the ranch decorated the same way, the meal rotations on the same schedule, and—"

"I know, Bree." Brody squeezed her hand.

"But I'm not her. I'm never going to be her. I'm never going to be able to quilt and mend things the way she did, or decorate, or plant and tend the roses...or control my horrible temper. She was so sweet and loved by everybody and—"

"You're trying too hard," Brody cut in. He reached the base of the hill and pulled into the gravel parking lot in front of the ancient white church house. The paint was peeling and the pair of blue urns on the front porch had been stripped free of their leaves and blooms by the relentless winds whistling down the hillside. "Nobody can do it on their own."

Bree brushed at the dampness beneath her eyes. "What do you mean?"

"Mom taught you a lot more than her family-secret recipes, Bree. She did more than show you how to sew and take care of the rest of us at the ranch. If you had to pick out the single biggest thing she and Pops taught us, what would it be?"

Bree closed her eyes to block out the brightness

of the morning sun spilling over the church grounds. "To have faith." She hardly knew what it meant, but it was the thing their parents had talked about the most often.

"Bingo."

"I haven't wanted to think about stuff like that after they left us. It's too hard."

His expression turned curious. "What's so hard about it?"

"Believing gives you hope. And when you get your hopes up, they're always doomed to come crashing back down."

"Only if you put your hope in the wrong things."

"Or the wrong people," she added bitterly.

"That, too, but we'll circle back to the topic of our new ranch manager in a minute. Right now I'd like to focus on the kind of hope Mom and Pops had, because I think it's the one thing that'll make you feel better."

"How?" She spread her hands. "I don't even know where to begin."

"Sure you do. Sometimes you just get discouraged and need to be reminded. Come with me." He pushed open his door. "I'll show you."

As expected, he led her across the church parking lot to the cemetery, where they strolled to the white stone markers in front of Mom and Pops' graves. As they paused there, she felt close to dissolving into tears again.

"I didn't bring you here to make you any sadder

than you already are, Bree. I brought you here to remind you of something."

She turned streaming eyes to him. "Of how much we've lost?" she cried piteously. They'd lost so crazy much — their birth parents, their adoptive parents, most of their savings to her unscrupulous ex, not to mention her dignity and pride. Then there was the mortgage on the ranch they often struggled to pay, which meant they could lose that, too, at any point. And don't even get her started on Brody's horseback riding accident that had left him a cripple. He desperately needed to return to physical therapy, but that wasn't going to happen until they could get their finances back on track and start paying for health insurance again.

"Nope. I brought you here to remind you of how much we've gained." Brody's smile was infused with so much compassion and understanding that Bree almost wanted to slap him. He was forever brimming with such impossible optimism!

"I know our parents are no longer with us, but their passing didn't change the fact that they adopted us, Bree."

"Not saying it did."

"They gave us their last name and made us Andersons. They made us their family. And we're still all of those things."

"I know, Brody," she sighed. Man, but it was hard to stay mad while standing in the Texas breeze with the four of them together again. Even her headache seemed to be losing its oomph.

"They gave us more than their ranch, Bree. They gave us faith. They taught us to believe in something greater than ourselves. Remember what Mom always said?"

She nodded, blinking past tears. "Better days ahead."

"And Pops' favorite saying?"

"The best is yet to come." She gave a damp chuckle. "Well, technically, he had two favorite sayings. The other one was, everything happens for a reason."

"Like Matt Romero driving up that highway two weeks ago and being stopped for speeding, right when you needed his help."

Bree blinked at Brody's abrupt change in tone. "I really, really, really don't want to talk about that jerk."

"I know you don't, but maybe it would help if you knew why he was speeding."

She gritted her teeth. "I'm guessing it's because he was pushing down a little too hard on his gas pedal?"

"That's the science behind it, yes, but most people only do stuff like that when they're distracted."

"Or being careless and irresponsible."

"It was his wedding day, Bree. Or supposed to be," he amended sadly.

"Oh-h-h-h." She sucked in a breath. Well, that put things in a slightly different perspective.

"The woman on our back porch earlier talked him into leaving the military. But by the time he finished serving his final months of duty, she'd found someone else. Didn't even give him the courtesy of telling him. He found out by accident."

A lump of sickness formed in the pit of Bree's stomach. "She cheated on him?" Fury rolled across her tongue as she spoke the words. What kind of woman would cheat on a soldier who was in the middle of making such a big sacrifice for her? And Bree knew with a sudden certainly that Matt had done it willingly. He was just that kind of person. The kind that would risk his life to dive inside a smoking vehicle after a perfect stranger, just because it was the right thing to do. It made her shiver in wonder at the thought of how much more loyal he might be to someone he actually knew.

And loved.

"Yeah, and now she says she's sorry and wants him back."

"Oh. My. Lands!" Bree's voice rose in incredulity. "You don't just get to march back into someone's life and pick up where you left off after tearing it to pieces like that." She couldn't imagine how she would feel if Cory tried to do the same to her, but a few adjectives came to mind. Angry. Bitter. Murderous.

"No, you don't, Bree, and I don't think he plans to let her. He's too smart for that."

She bit her lower lip in contemplation as she

mulled the details. "She's still wearing a pretty big rock on her hand."

"So he's not the kind of guy to demand back a gift once it's given. That just makes him the Matt we've come to know so well. Generous to a fault. Doesn't mean he plans to return his heart and loyalty to a woman not worth giving it to. Like you, he learned a hard lesson. One he won't soon forget."

Convincing Bree that Matt didn't plan to get back together with his ex wasn't the only reason Brody had driven them to the cemetery. Or even the main reason. But Bree's heart felt much lighter at the knowledge, anyway. If Matt was still at the ranch when they got back, she might be able to dig up a little faith. And start believing again in better days ahead. Heaven knew he was the biggest shot their ranch had at seeing better days.

Brody drove her back home in silence. The fact that he never felt the need to fill up every nook and cranny of silence was one of the things she loved best about her brother. Her headache was almost gone, and she no longer felt like crying. As they pulled up the driveway leading to the house, however, her heartbeat started to race all over again.

The yellow Corvette was gone, but Matt wasn't. He was leaning against one of the thick, white porch columns with his arms crossed, like he'd been waiting for their return, and he was still wearing that ridiculous black mask. As Brody halted the truck and trailer, Matt jogged down the steps two at a time.

He made a beeline for Bree's side of the truck to open the door. Then he reached for her.

She placed her hands on his shoulders and allowed him to swing her down, which he did ever so gently.

"How's your head?" He sounded so strained that she knew he'd been genuinely worried about her.

"Take off the mask," she commanded softly.

He went still for a moment. Then he reached up to remove it.

She grimaced at the creases that remained on his cheeks and nose, along with the beads of perspiration dotting his forehead. Heaven help her, but it wasn't the first time this guy had sweated because of her. "I don't want to see that thing again until Halloween." She fanned a hand at his face. "Maybe not even then." She wasn't sure she'd ever be able to rid her memories of his mean-spirited ex kissing him with it on.

"Okay." He caught her hand and lowered it between them, lacing his fingers through hers. A concerned scowl wrinkled his forehead. "She's gone, Bree. For good."

Her heart raced at the delicious knowledge that Matt Romero was making it clear to her that he was very single again and very available.

She bit her lower lip. "About what you asked me earlier, I want those double ovens stacked on one side with at least three warming drawers stacked right next to them."

"Done." His dark gaze burned into hers,

promising things that neither of them were ready to voice just yet.

She found she wasn't in all that big of a hurry to head back to the house or office yet. She was too busy trying to remember why she'd ever thought Matt Romero was hard to look at.

Holy hotness! The guy who'd saved her life was a thousand shades of gorgeous. A man with a heart of pure gold, and the kind of loyalty she'd only dreamed of inspiring in another person.

The way he was looking at her was making it harder to think. And breathe. All she wanted was to stand there for the next few hundred years with his beautiful eyes promising her better days ahead between them.

CHAPTER 6: CANES AND CONSTRUCTION
Matt

"A little help over here?" Brody called.

At the urgency in his voice, Matt dropped Bree's hand and sprinted around the back of the trailer. She followed.

Brody's face was contorted in pain as he hopped in a strange little dance while trying to hold the reins of the spirited horse he'd just led from the trailer.

"What's going on?" Matt reached for the reins and patted the horse's neck, making a few soothing sounds to quiet her prancing.

Bree stooped to pick up the cane her brother had dropped and handed it back to him.

"It's this stupid leg of mine." Brody was bent nearly double, though he was able to use the cane to regain his balance. "Cramping like you wouldn't believe. It's been getting worse ever since I stopped going to physical therapy a few months ago."

Now, why would you do a thing like—? Ah. Matt's heart sank at what Brody left unsaid. Now that he was thinking about it, there were no health insurance premiums listed as a line item on the ranch's monthly budget. Which probably explained why Brody had made so many trips between the police department and the hospital billing office while Bree was in the hospital. He'd been making sure her medical expenses were covered by the party responsible for the collision.

"Listen." Matt cast a sideways glance at his friend and business partner. "I have zero interest in prying into your personal stuff, but I might know someone who could put together a PT regimen you could follow on your own. He'd need you to describe your injury to him in as much detail as possible, of course."

"No problem," Brody wheezed, flexing his leg a few times and panting his way through the cramps. When he finally straightened, he was several shades paler than before. "What happened to me is no state secret. He can have copies of my x-rays, whatever he needs."

"Brody got thrown from his horse during a stampede," Bree supplied bitterly. "We still haven't figured out what happened that day. All we know is that a pair of bulls came charging like demons straight through the fence, and..." She bit her lower lip, which was trembling. "Short version is Brody got wrapped around a tree, the horse took off, and the herd following behind the bulls parted and thundered around him on both sides." She drew a deep breath before continuing. "In the end, the same tree that mangled his leg was what saved his life."

Matt's jaw dropped. It sounded to him like it was a miracle Brody was alive. No wonder the guy believed that some things were simply meant to be. "If you'll get me those x-rays, I'll send 'em to my friend and see what he says."

"Just let me catch my breath. Then I'll go raid my medical file." Brody offered a two-fingered salute as Matt finished leading the horse toward the barn.

Excitement prickled in his gut over the possibility that his friend in physical therapy might be able to help Brody. Brody was one of those rare, amazing guys in the universe who was simply worth helping. Matt was also glad for the opportunity to be able to do something that might actually stand a chance at impressing Bree. Man, but he had it bad for her!

It was too soon to make any moves, of course. He didn't want Bree to think she was merely someone for him to snag on the rebound, nor did he wish for her to get the impression he wasn't capable of standing on his own feet emotionally. He would remain single until he was sure he had his head screwed on straight again. When he finally asked her out, the timing was going to be right.

"Yooo, there!" Harley's shout interrupted Matt's reverie. He looked up to see the older ranch hand striding his way across the gravel path. "I need to hit the trail soon, so I'll take her from here."

"No problem." Matt gladly handed off the mare into Harley's care. He certainly didn't mind getting out of the tasks of feeding and brushing her down.

"So, what did you have to do to bring 'er back? Hog tie the little filly?" Harley cocked one bushy gray brow at him.

It took a moment for Matt to register the fact that Harley wasn't referring to the horse, but rather to Bree. He grinned. "Actually, Brody is the one who went after her."

"The priestly brother," Crew drawled, coming up from behind Harley. They were standing in front of the big red barn behind the ranch house. Under Matt's orders, the men were busy emptying it out and relocating all the animals and supplies to the two smaller barns out back. One was a weathered gray building that could use a coat of paint, and the other was a newer, white steel structure. Matt and Harley had been debating the odds of either adding on to it or raising a second steel structure nearby.

"Guess you're right." Matt's lips twitched at Crew's words. He couldn't deny the fact that Brody was about as close to a saint as a guy could get.

"Ol' Pops was the same way." Crew's voice took on a cynical ring. "Like my mother always used to say..."

At Matt's interested look, he bit off whatever it was that his mother used to say, presumably about

Pops, leaving Matt to wonder what the connection was between the cowboy's mother and Brody's adoptive father. He made a mental note to dig a little farther into the guy's personnel file to see what might surface, if anything.

"Walk with me, Crew." Matt fell into step between the two men. "I wouldn't mind an update on our progress in prepping the barn for renovations."

Harley tipped his dusty Stetson and veered away from them to head toward the white steel barn about a hundred yards away. "As soon as you're done with yer briefing," Harley tossed over his shoulder, "I could use a riding partner out on the trail."

"Count me in, Har." Crew waved his response, looking a little nervous in Matt's opinion.

It wasn't the first time he'd gotten the impression that Harley was trying to minimize the time he spent alone in Crew's presence. The feeling grew that Crew was hiding something from him, along with the nagging suspicion that Harley might be in on whatever it was.

"Did we finish getting all the hay bales moved?" he prodded to get the cowboy talking again.

Crew nodded and pushed back his hat as they entered the barn. "Nash and Zane set up a hydraulic pulley to lower them from the loft straight to the truck." There was a hint of pride in his voice at their ingenuity. "We also kept both tractors going, because why not? Throw a double hay spike on the end, and you can get things done a lot faster than sitting around and waiting for the truck to return."

"Appreciate all you guys have been doing for the past few days." Matt meant it, too. Emptying out the barn was a massive undertaking, definitely not a one-man show.

"Hey, you ordered the pizza and hot wings." Crew shrugged companionably. "Guess you figured out there's not much we won't do for food."

"You and me both, man." Matt was a little surprised at the pleasant turn their conversation had taken. Normally, Crew was more closed-mouthed around him, bordering on hostile, even.

"So you're serious about turning this place into a hotel and restaurant, huh?" Crew spun around the near-empty main hall of the barn. It was a wide-open area, complete with a concrete floor and a three-story cathedral roof, about the size of a basketball court.

"I am." Matt gestured to include the front part of the room. "You'll enter into a guest lounge that'll serve as the waiting room for the restaurant, as well as the reception area for the hotel. From there, you'll step inside the restaurant, which will contain a mix of round tables and booth seating. The far end of the room will house a stage with theater lighting and backdrops, that'll allow us to transform the barn for larger events, as needed — weddings, parties, dinner theaters, and the like." On one side of the hall would be the kitchen, laundry and housekeeping service, and linen storage area. Plus, there would be a small indoor gym with a heated pool and spa. The other side of the hall would house four first-floor guest suites. An additional eight suites would be built into the loft areas, four on each side of the barn, for a grand total of twelve guest suites.

It was a spacious layout with lots of luxury accommodations wrapped in a rustic lodge theme that Bree was hard at work designing. Matt glanced around the room, already picturing the antler chandeliers and iron pendant lights she'd picked out, as well as the horse saddle stools, boot spur curtain rods, mountains of country quilts and embroidered linens, and the list went on and on. The most amazing part about it was that Bree was gathering a good amount of those items for next to nothing in the way of an investment — raiding second-hand shops right and left to find things she could refurbish or utterly transform.

She was turning out to be a veritable magician with a thread and needle. Add in a glue gun, hammer, and a paintbrush, and the woman was literally unstoppable. She was even tossing the idea around about opening a small gift shop in the entry foyer — a place to sell homemade candles and soaps, aprons and hand towels, as well as a collection of jams, jellies, and preserves. He was her biggest fan, unable to find one idea of hers that he couldn't fully get behind. His only concern, whatsoever, was overworking her.

"Well, uh..." Matt didn't realize how long he'd been silent until Crew's awkward drawl interrupted his thoughts. "I guess I'll be getting back outside to help Harley."

"One more thing before you go." Matt hated the way the wiry cowboy's shoulders tensed at his words. "Have you given any thought about where you plan to fit into our new line of business? Any particular role you'd like to take on or train for?" The guy might be a high school dropout, but he was a crazy hard worker and a quick learner. No matter how many tasks Matt and Harley threw at him, he always got them done.

Crew snorted. "In case you missed that part of my file, I don't have much in the way of credentials."

"Is that something you're looking to change?" Matt had been waiting for just the right opportunity to bring up the topic about Crew's education.

"Not particularly." Crew's tanned features grew shuttered. "Why? Is that some new requirement you're going to throw at us?" He grimaced. "Must have a high school diploma to darken the door of your fancy shmancy hotel?"

"No, but if you're gunning for a management position someday..." Matt let that settle between them for a moment.

"Me?" Crew barked out a laugh. "Management? Get real."

"Why not?" Matt scowled at him. "You're getting in on the ground floor of something that could grow into something big someday."

"I don't know." Crew gave a huff of derision, trying to look like he didn't care, though Matt could tell that he'd given him something to chew on. "Guess I'm what you'd call a jack-of-all-trades. Your go-to guy when you need something fixed. A cowboy, range rider in the making, farmer, repairman..."

Matt shrugged, trying to sound casual. "Sounds like a future head of maintenance in the making to me. Just saying. So if you decide you want to go for your G.E.D. at some point, or get a few college classes under your belt the way Bree is doing, just let me know, alright? We'll work out something in the way of a job benefit to cover the expense."

Crew's upper lip curled. "Why would you do that?"

"Because the more you improve yourself, the more valuable of an employee you'll become." Matt's lips twitched as he prepared to drive home the money shot, literally. "And the bigger raises I'll be able to consider come evaluation time."

Crew's eyes bugged out at that, and he seemed to be at a loss for words. It was one of those rare moments when he wasn't smirking or giving Matt an attitude, which felt like a win.

"Just think about it," he urged. "No hurry. My door's always open if you want to talk." With that, he continued striding across the hall to check on Nash and Zane Wilder. The roguish cowboy brothers were in their early to mid-twenties, fraternal twins according to Harley. Unlike Crew, they had their high school diplomas. Like Crew, however, they didn't seem to have any major college or career aspirations outside of life on the ranch.

"Looks like you've finished transporting the hay," Matt called out by way of a greeting to them.

Nash was munching on a piece of straw while examining a loose wooden stair leading up to the lofts. His gray eyes twinkled at Matt's approach. He was one of those guys who always looked like he was about to start laughing, even when he wasn't. "Sure did. We'll need to get back to our regular duties on the farm in a bit, but we could probably start spraying insulation by tomorrow morning." He switched his piece of straw from one side of his mouth to the other. "Assuming you're ready for us to move forward with that."

"Works for me." Matt was pleased to hear that they were a full two days ahead of schedule. "Have either of you given any thought to what roles you'd like to take on or train for with the hotel?"

Nash and Zane traded startled looks. "We're farmers, Matt." Zane reminded in his quiet baritone. "We drive tractors, bale hay, and harvest crops."

Nash's mouth quirked at the corners as he stabbed his thumb in Zane's direction. "He's too modest to admit it, but we're also working on getting our pilot licenses, so we can run a crop duster."

Matt made a mental note of that. If things continued the way he, Brody, and Bree hoped, they'd be expanding their herd in a year or two. That, in turn, would require them to grow more hay, wheat, corn, and alfalfa, which might eventually justify the cost of investing in their own crop dusting jet.

"Hey, Mr. Ranch Manager!" Bree's voice echoed like music to Matt's ears across the empty building.

Every cell in his body became instantly more aware as he spun around. His mouth went dry at the sight of her in a sundress. It was the first time he'd seen her in anything besides jeans.

Falling just above the knee, it was a white cotton thing dotted with tiny red rosebuds. Her legs were still encased in her favorite beige leather boots, however, and a matching Stetson was perched at a sassy angle on her head. Instead of her usual braid, though, her long strawberry blonde hair hung freely down her back.

"You need something, darlin'?" The endearment slipped out before he could think about what he was saying.

Nash glanced up from the stair he was tinkering with as Bree stepped over a two-by-four and made her way in their direction. "Is it my imagination, or is the boss lady in a dress?"

Zane chuckled as he handed his brother a few nails. "Up 'til this very moment, I didn't think she owned one."

"Did I miss a holiday or something?" Nash joked with a sly look in Matt's direction. "Can't think of any other good reason to dress up on a regular ol' Saturday. Can you, bro?"

Zane chuckled again. "I think she has a college class mid-afternoon."

"Nope." Nash shook his head emphatically. "Don't think I can recall her ever dressing up for a college class. Not the entire time we've been employed here. Must be some other reason she decided to go shopping all of a sudden."

Wishing they'd put a sock in it, Matt stepped away from the two brothers as Bree drew closer.

She waved a big white envelope as she reached him. "I've gotta head to class soon, but here are those records Brody said he'd get to you."

Matt accepted the envelope, drinking in how pretty she looked in her dress. He experienced the sudden urge to close the short distance between them to lay a kiss on her. "Do you need a ride to class?"

"Aww!" Nash cooed from behind them, making Matt wish he had something to throw at him.

Though Bree gave no indication she'd heard him, pink blossomed in her cheeks. "Actually, I was hoping for a quick tour of my future kitchen," she confessed, turning even pinker.

Matt liked the fact that her request required them to walk out of earshot from the Wilder brothers.

"There," Bree noted in relief as they stepped inside the paved room that would eventually become the hotel kitchen. "I didn't want to say this in front of Nash and Zane, because Brody's a pretty private person but I'm worried about him, Matt." Her voice held a breathless quality.

"Talk to me," he commanded softly.

She was standing so close that all he'd have to do is take one more step to bring them into kissing distance.

Worry made her blue eyes appear darker. "At the rate he's losing his mobility, I'm afraid he's going to end up in a wheelchair soon." She made a moaning sound. "I think it would kill him, absolutely kill him! So, please help me fix him."

"I'm going to do everything I can, babe." He mentally vowed to personally oversee Brody's therapy. Maybe they could work out together in the mornings or evenings or something.

"If you get him off that cane, I swear there's a kiss in it for you." Her blue eyes sparkled with a poignant mix of pleading laced with promise.

Matt was thoroughly entranced. There was only one proper answer to a statement like that. He drew his phone out of his pocket in one smooth motion. Holding her gaze, he dialed his friend who worked as a physical therapist at Ft. Benning. To his surprise and relief, Benjiro Taniguchi picked up on the second ring.

"Matt!" he crowed. "How in the heck are you?"

"Never better!" Matt grinned, wishing he could see the look on his friend's face when he told him why he was calling. "Just calling to collect that favor you owe me."

"Always knew you would. How many bodies we gonna have to bury this time?"

"Only one, but I don't think he's ready to go six feet under just yet. What we're gunning for is a PT regimen that'll keep him out of a wheelchair."

"Sounds serious." His friend quickly sobered. "Give me the low-down."

"Riding accident." Matt grimaced as he shared what he knew about Brody's muscle cramps and the increasing loss of his range in motion. "I'll scan and email you his x-rays within the hour."

"I'll be on the lookout for 'em. As for my preliminary take on the situation..." He paused.

"Listening."

"Assuming the bones are properly healed, we're likely dealing with some ongoing muscular and tendon retracting and tightening. Without proper therapy, they'll continue to freeze up and cost him his range in motion."

"Makes sense."

"I take it we're dealing with a lack of medical insurance."

"Yep."

"Figured that. So here's what I can do. We'll map out a comprehensive set of stretching exercises combined with heat therapy. Some of this stuff he's going to need to keep doing, as in forever."

"I'll let him in on that fun bit of news."

"Any chance you're in the position to work out with him?"

"Absolutely."

"Then I'll include some mobilizations for you to step him through. He'll get better sooner and ditch that cane faster, if you can apply the kind of weights and pressures to the area I'll be coaching you through."

"I can't thank you enough." Excitement shot through Matt's chest at Ben's words. He made it sound like Brody's condition was not only treatable, but curable with ongoing therapy.

"No need. I owe you, remember?"

"Time frame?" Matt inquired quickly.

"Sometime today. Not sure when, but it'll be before I catch any shut-eye."

"Haven't lost your coolness, Ben."

"Yep, I'm the best, bro. Aw, snap!" There was a loud beeping sound in the background. "Getting another page. Gotta run, but you know how to get ahold of me if you need anything else."

"Thanks again." Matt disconnected the call.

Bree had been watching him anxiously. "Well? Your side of the conversation sure had a positive ring to it."

"He said he'll have something to us by the end of the day." He held her gaze, not wanting to miss any nuance of her response to what he was about to say. "Brody won't be going into a chair." As she caught her breath, he added, "If everything goes the way my friend hopes, he might even be able to ditch the cane."

"Matt!" she whispered, her gorgeous blue eyes glinting with sudden emotion. Without warning, she stepped closer to touch her mouth to his.

She was the second woman who'd kissed him today, but the only one who mattered. He slid an arm around her waist to cuddle her closer. Heart pounding at her nearness, he reveled in her sweet sass, her crazy good scent, and her hard-won acceptance — something he'd only dreamed of earning before he was old and gray.

"What's this for?" he muttered when she tipped her face back a few inches to stare up at him. "I thought you were going to make me wait." *At least a million years.*

"Changed my mind," she informed him breathlessly. "Sometimes I do that."

"Not complaining." She was every bit as wonderful to be with as he dreamed she would be, and her kiss had matched her temperament — unpredictable, exciting, fierce, and possessive. She was an all-or-nothing kind of girl. Someone who didn't trust easily or give her loyalty lightly. The fact that she was finally giving both of those things to him took the breath right out of his chest.

Something shifted between them. Something monumentally important and wonderful. Something he swore on the spot he would never give up. Never walk away from. Something he would spend the rest of his life trying to be worthy of.

She cupped his cheek as she stepped back.

"Maybe that'll help you forget the heart stomping you took earlier from that mean girl."

He waggled his brows at her. "Who?" he teased, dizzy with the joy of knowing Bree Anderson had just agreed, in so many words, to be his girl.

"Good answer." She drew his head down for another kiss.

CHAPTER 7: FIERY DISASTER
Bree

The next morning, Bree took her coffee break extra early on the side porch overlooking the east forty acres. It no longer felt like an invasion of her privacy if Matt caught sight of her in the filmy short-sleeved hoodie and yoga pants she'd just finished stretching out in. No running yet, per doctor's orders. She seriously couldn't wait to get back to her morning jogs and trail rides. In addition to sipping coffee, she liked to start her mornings by breaking a sweat and pumping endorphins. Exercise always made her feel better for the rest of the day.

A sense of satisfaction crept over her at the knowledge that the two enormous breakfast ring casseroles she'd cooked the evening before were slowly heating in the oven. The scent of yeast from the croissants wafted through the window she'd left cracked for the fresh air while she was working. Combined with the warm swirl of almond coffee fumes, it was a heavenly smell, one that made her feel better than she had since the afternoon of her nightmarish accident. Nearly one hundred percent back to her old self. Or not.

After what had happened between her and Matt yesterday, she was pretty sure some things in her life were never going back to the way they were. She smiled as she took another sip of coffee, reliving the magic of being in his embrace. In the next moment, however, her rosy memories were marred by the fury of having to watch his ex march up the back porch stairs and pretend like she had the right to kick him aside and take him back at will. Like she owned him or something.

Bree closed her eyes against the flash of the massive diamond she'd been waving around. Gosh, but Matt didn't hold back! She didn't want to even think about how much a stone like that must've cost him — on a soldier's salary, no less.

A part of her was worried that she'd kissed him too soon. Yesterday was only two weeks past the day he was supposed to get married. But the moment had felt right. More importantly, he'd kissed her back.

Which didn't keep her from sensing the thick waves of sadness coursing through him. And regret. And the fear of making another mistake. Sentiments she understood all too well. Yeah, he was attracted to her, but she needed to protect what was happening between them with everything she had in her. Like her, he needed time to nurse his wounds. To heal. To rebuild. And then. Only then. Maybe.

She closed her eyes as she leaned her head against one of the porch columns, breathing in the peace of the morning and soaking in the warmth of the first rays breaking over the horizon. This was why she loved this particular spot so much. It was where she got to wake up with the day. Where she got to experience a new beginning with each and every sunrise.

"Hey, you." The light scrape of a footstep against the sidewalk was the only indication that she hadn't imagined Matt's voice. Or conjured it up from the most precious parts of her memories.

She opened her eyes and glanced toward the sound. He was standing just outside the screened-in porch with his face tipped up to hers.

"Morning," she answered softly, drinking in the sight of him in his plain gray v-neck shirt, black running shorts, and sneakers. A clean white sweat towel was tossed across his shoulder, along with a colored set of stretchy bands. She wondered if he was heading for the gym that the ranch hands had set up in one of the storage rooms of the big steel barn. The guys were forever dragging used and refurbished pieces of equipment into the place to tinker back into mint condition.

"Didn't want to startle you and make you spill your coffee." He quirked a smile at her that warmed her all the way to her toes.

She smiled back. "It's a good rule to live by. Never

mess with a gal holding a mug of her favorite scalding beverage."

"Truth." He gave her a mocking salute but seemed in no hurry to take off.

She took another sip, liking the way he was looking at her and liking how special it made her feel. "So do you want to talk about it, soldier?"

"About?"

"Our kiss."

He glanced away. "We probably should."

"It was just a kiss, Matt."

His head whipped back to hers, his gaze darkening. "What are you saying, Bree?"

"I'm saying I don't expect you to go claw that rock off your ex's finger and smash it onto mine."

He snorted. "You never say what I'm expecting. I'll give you that."

In for a penny. Since he seemed willing to listen, there were a few more things she wanted to get off her chest. "From the moment I woke from my coma, I didn't want you here. Didn't want you in our lives. Didn't want you on our ranch."

"No kidding!" He raised his brows. "Could've fooled me."

She chuckled. "I know it's a horribly unkind, uncharitable thing to say, but I didn't want you to be the guy who saved my life, either. Didn't want another newcomer crashing his way into Brody's trust. And I most definitely didn't want to have to look at you every day and finally face the things I've never finished dealing with."

He shook his head at her. "You don't need to apologize. I get what you're going through. Trust me."

"Oh, but I do need to apologize. I had no right to use you as my emotional punching bag, and I don't plan to do it anymore. Brody sort of set me straight on a few things yesterday. You know how he is. Anyway, he made me want to try harder to be a better version of me."

"Apology accepted, but don't change too much." He winked at her. "I kind of like you the way you are."

"Thanks." She felt suddenly shy. It felt good to be forgiven. It also felt really good not to be enemies with their ranch manager any longer.

"So did the beard help?" He reached up to rub a hand over his scruffy jawline. "Back at the hospital, Brody warned me how much I looked like a ghost from your past, and that it might be a problem when you woke up. I was hoping the beard might help."

She hugged her coffee mug to her chest. "You being you, Matt. That's what helped the most."

"Well, that's certainly something I can keep doing." He shot her a wicked grin. "So what's it going to be? Beard or no beard for our next kiss?"

"Who said I was going to kiss you again?" It felt right to tap on the brakes between them. Not too hard, just hard enough to give him the space he needed. The space they both needed right now. She promised him with her eyes that she was keeping all possibilities on the table, though.

"I take it you're going to make me work even harder for the next one."

"I have my reasons." She reached out to splay her hand against the screen. "But I don't mind sharing this. The next time you kiss me, it won't be the same day you kissed another woman."

"I didn't kiss her back." He stepped closer to press his hand to hers through the screen.

But his ex had still managed to mess with his head, open up old wounds, and make him hurt all over again. Bree's heart ached for him. "I kissed you because you were hurting and I was hurting. I wanted us both to have something else to think about. But next time needs to be different. Just us."

"Agreed."

Her heartbeat raced at the realization he was just as determined as she was that there was going to be a next time. "I'll have breakfast ready soon if you care to join us." He'd missed a lot of their gatherings, though she'd nearly always caught sight of him later on eating a hasty sandwich or granola bar on the go. No doubt it was because he'd been trying so hard to avoid yet another awkward encounter with her. Well, those days were behind them. It was time for him to quit avoiding her.

"I'll be there, chef."

The timer on her watch chimed. "Time to go fresh-squeeze the orange juice." She tapped her fingers against his one last time before turning away.

Matt finished making his way to the gym that the ranch hands had set up in the white barn. It was, by far, not the most upscale space he'd ever worked out in, but it had all the key and essential items. There were two benches with bars and free weights, a squat machine, and a full set of dumbbells. There was even a three-level steel tower for pull-ups, dips, and planks.

Because farmers and ranchers got up at the crack of dawn, the other guys did most of their working out in the evenings. That's why Matt had set up today's appointment with Brody so bright and early. Since he'd arrived a few minutes before their agreed-upon time, he got busy setting up their workspace according to Ben's specifications.

It was a gym instead of a physical therapy unit, so there were no raised booths to work with. He settled for rolling out a set of mats he found in an unlocked storage cabinet in the corner of the room.

Brody hobbled in on his cane only seconds later. "I see you've got the torture chamber all set up."

"No pain, no gain," Matt retorted cheerfully, rubbing his hands together in mock anticipation. Since he'd dealt with a torn Achilles a few years ago, he was more familiar than he wanted to be with the science behind physical therapy. It hurt, but it worked, plain and simple.

"Let's just get it over with," Brody sighed. It was the first time Matt had seen him in anything besides jeans and boots, so the sight of his scars was a little shocking. They crisscrossed both the front and the back of his leg.

According to Brody's surgical records that Matt and Ben had discussed in detail, Brody had fractured his right thighbone, the strongest bone in a person's leg, while additionally shattering both his kneecap and fibula. It had taken multiple surgeries and a few titanium pins to correct.

Matt pulled out his phone to dial Ben, who'd so kindly agreed to coach them through their first session.

"Yo, man!" the therapist sang out. "You got our victim all strung out on the rack, I hope?"

Matt mashed another button to turn on his video feed. Then he propped the screen against his rolled towel on the nearest weight bench, giving Ben the full view of their work area.

"I heard that," Brody growled. "So you're the PT guy Matt has been talking about."

Ben waved two fingers. "Specializing in human torture for eight years straight. You bend it, tear it, or break it, and I can help you fix it. All it costs is a little time and pain. Sometimes a lot of pain." He didn't look overly concerned about that last detail.

"Gee, thanks for sugar-coating it for me." Under

Ben's direction, Brody laid flat on his back on top of the rubber mat, and Matt knelt beside him.

They started off with a few easy repetitions that Matt soon realized was merely to help Ben figure out what Brody's current range of motion was with his damaged leg. Sadly, it didn't take much action to send him into his first gut-wrenching spasm.

"As expected, we have our work cut out for us." Ben's Asian features were set in stoic lines as he dispassionately surveyed Brody's doubled-up figure. Though Ben had always been good at hiding his emotions, the look in his eyes told Matt that his professional empathy was very much engaged with his patient's current pain level. That didn't mean he planned to go easy on him, though. Far from it.

By the time Ben was finished with their first session, Brody was white-faced and panting on the mat. "Well, nobody said this was going to be easy," he groaned, propping one arm over his eyes.

"Nope," Ben agreed, "but that's not why you reached out to me, is it?"

"Got a ranch to run," Brody muttered. "Can't do what I do if I end up in a chair."

"But that's not your only reason," Ben returned smoothly, "or your biggest one, eh?"

When Brody didn't answer, Ben kept talking. "I've watched a lot of men and women muscle their way through a lot of pain during my sessions, but there's a certain look I run into sometimes. A look that says a patient isn't here for himself. They're pushing to get well for someone else. Not trying to pry, but whoever she is, you hang on to her every time you and I meet."

"Oh, yay! You mean we actually get to do this again?" Though Brody was still panting, Matt could hear the immense gratitude in his voice. He was pretty sure Ben heard it, too.

"When I'm pushing you past points you don't think you can bear," Ben continued sternly, "you picture her face and keep giving our workouts everything you've got."

"Okay, but why are you doing this?" Brody pushed himself to a sitting position with a groan. "I know Matt said you owed him a favor, but this feels a little beyond that."

Ben cocked his thumb and forefinger like a pistol. "Okay, you caught me. I'm trying out some new therapy jazz on you. You agree to continue being my guinea pig, and I'll do it for free. That's the deal. Take it, or leave it."

"Taking it." Brody gave him a weary wave. "But if it works, this guinea pig is still going to feel like he owes you. An Anderson always pays his debts."

Ben's dark eyes twinkled. "It'll work, so prepare to owe me. I hear you're about to open up a steak restaurant, so I'm sure we can work something out."

"We can." A faint smile eased the tightness in Brody's features. "Appreciate you letting me open a tab like this. I'm sure you've probably figured out it's the only way I'm going to be able to afford your services."

"No problem, but I'll have to skip the group hug, since my next appointment started ten minutes ago. Ciao for now." With a waggle of his dark brows, the screen went blank.

"Bree invited me to breakfast." To distract Brody from his soreness, Matt started talking again. Though he knew Bree wasn't ready to be his girlfriend in public, he wanted to give Brody the satisfaction of knowing things were getting better between the two of them.

"Oh, wow! That's progress." Brody ran a hand through his short-clipped dark hair, then curled to his feet with a huff of pain. "She and I had a long overdue heart-to-heart yesterday. She's lost a lot of people she cares for. Makes her afraid to get attached to anyone new."

"Sorta picked up on that."

"I appreciate your continued patience with her. She's worth the wait, Matt. Promise you that."

"If that's your way of asking if I'm here for the long haul, the answer is yes." With every passing day, Matt was starting to buy more and more into Brody's blind faith that everything happened for a reason.

Though Bree's struggle with accepting him hadn't been fun to endure over the past couple of weeks, it had turned into one of the most motivating and inspiring things in his adult life. Just hearing her talk about wanting to be a better version of herself, made him want to do the same.

He'd spent way too much time lately being angry,

hurt, and resentful. Maybe he had a right to be, but that wasn't the point. Those kinds of emotions were too toxic to hang onto for long. If someone who'd been through as much as Bree could let go of the hurt and pain, then so could he. They would do it together. And when they succeeded, the better version of him was totally going to ask out the better version of her.

He jogged the short distance back to his cabin for the additional workout, since he'd spent most of his gym session spotting Brody instead of getting much exercise, himself. He really liked the guy and hoped they could eventually do some real workouts together. But for now, he was content to focus on Bree's request to fix her brother.

He saw the swirl of gray and smelled the smoke well before he completed his uphill trek. *No way!* He sprinted the rest of the way up the hill to discover the cabin where he'd been staying was completely consumed with flames. For a moment, all Matt could do was stare with his hands clasped on top of his head. Everything he owned was inside those four walls. His collection of electronics, all of his military gear, his entire wardrobe, and his few mementos. *Gone!* All of it gone.

The only possession he had on his person, besides one sweaty towel, was his wallet and keys. Without wasting any more time, he sprinted for his truck, leaped inside, and gunned it down Sidewinder Canyon. He drove as fast as he safely could while keeping all four wheels on the gravel. Laying on his horn, he circled the driveway in front of the main ranch and skidded to a halt.

Before his feet hit the ground, he was dialing 911. He reported the fire and headed inside to the dining room where the ranch staff was gathering for breakfast.

"Fire!" he shouted, catching sight of Harley first. He was seated at the foot of the table. "My cabin's up in flames, and it'll spread to the trees next, then the cornfields. I don't know how long it'll take for the fire department to get here. We gotta hold it off."

Crew, who'd been sipping on coffee while lounging next to Harley, leaped to his feet, looking horrified. "I'll rattle Nash and Zane's chains. They were last in line for the shower."

Just as Matt and Harley were making their exit, Bree flew into the dining room with a large breakfast casserole in hand. "Did someone say fire?" Her concerned gaze fixed on Matt as she hastily set the dish in the middle of the table on a pair of hot pads.

"It's the cabin." He shoved a hand through his hair, thoroughly confused. "I don't know what could've started it. I don't smoke. I didn't leave anything plugged in. Haven't once turned on the stove." He hated the fact that the cabin she and her brother had so kindly lent to him was about to be utterly destroyed. Not to mention the many memories of their adoptive father they'd kept stored there — countless hunting photos, his fishing supplies, a few mounted deer heads, and all sorts of old quilts and other items that no doubt held great personal value.

Ignoring his frustrated rambling, Bree ran up to him for a closer look. Resting one hand on his chest, she peered anxiously into his eyes. "Are you hurt? Did you—?"

"No, I'm fine. Saw the smoke on my run up the hill, but it was too late to save anything by the time I got there. The whole place was already in flames." It made no sense, but they could sort through the how and the why later. Right now, they had the Anderson's crops and greenhouses to save. Gently lowering Bree's hand from his chest, Matt nodded for Harley to follow him.

As he and Harley jogged to the barn, the older cowboy issued a few terse instructions. "I'll drive Crew out to the east fields, and he can help me get the pivot irrigators going. We'll focus on that side of the property and hopefully create a wet barrier that'll hold off the flames. Nash and Zane can move the herd to safer ground."

"What about those portable hose reels?" Matt demanded. "How many do we have?" There was no way he was going to stand around and watch the other guys do all the heavy lifting. There had to be something he could to do to help.

"Three." Harley scowled in contemplation. "Might not hurt to have you and Brody hook a couple of 'em to the tractors and work on irrigating the perimeter around the ranch house and barns."

"Roger that. We'll work our way toward the west pastures." Hopefully, the fire department would be there by then.

"Keys are in the metal box inside the tack room," Harley called after him.

Matt waved to acknowledge Harley's words without breaking his stride. Inside the tack room, he found both the keys he was searching for, as well as a livid Crew on his cell phone.

"Somebody could've gotten hurt!" he raged into the mouthpiece. Catching sight of Matt, he paled but continued to listen to whatever was being said on the other end of the line. "Guess I'll just have to go back to jail then," he snarled in response. "Do your worst. I'm out." Instead of hanging up the phone, he flung it across the room. It shattered into tiny pieces against the wall.

Matt scowled. "Dude, can it wait? We have a fire to fight."

"Yes," Crew growled, stomping past him. The look he gave Matt would've peeled the top layer of skin off of a weaker person. "And when it's over, I happen to know who started your blasted fire."

"Whoa!" Matt leaped in front of him so quickly that they nearly collided. "What's going on?"

"A fire, in case you've forgotten." Crew tried to shove past him, but Matt stopped him.

"Start talking, Crew."

"No time. Harley's going to need my help with those pivot irrigators. He's too old to do it by himself." Crew pulled a pistol from behind his back and held it out to Matt. "Short version is I broke parole, someone found out, and they've been blackmailing me into sharing our range riding schedules and a number of other things. The stuff that's gone missing is my fault. The fire is my fault. Everything is my fault, because I'm a screw up."

"What's the gun for, Crew?" Matt hated the fact that he'd been right about the cowboy having something to hide, but it was beginning to sound like Crew wasn't the one he truly needed to be worried about.

"Rattlesnakes, usually, or anything else that might harm the livestock."

"Then you better keep it on hand, just in case." Matt shoved it back into his hands.

Crew's upper lip curled. "Did you miss the part about me breaking parole? Guys like me aren't allowed to have guns. I'm a jail bird, bro. Not some freaking future head of maintenance at your fancy new hotel."

Matt scanned his features, liking the remorse and sincerity he saw there. "Right now I need you to be a cowboy, so take your gun and go help Harley. Then we'll see what we can do to get you out of whatever trouble you're in."

Crew gave a huff of disbelief and stuffed his pistol back in his waistband. "Not sure why you'd help a loser like me, but that's your problem."

"Yep, you became my problem the day I accepted the position of ranch manager. We're a team here at Anderson Ranch, and you're on that team. Now, go! I'm depending on you. We all are."

Still looking stunned, Crew took off at a sprint.

To Matt's relief, Crew did as he was told. Several times from his vantage point on the tractor, he caught sight of the cowboy helping Harley work the irrigation system across the cornfields. He wasn't running from his ranch duties, despite whatever mess he'd gotten himself in. So when the fire was put out, Matt wasn't going to run from his responsibilities toward Crew, either.

It was a good twenty minutes or so before the fire engine screamed its way up the driveway. Over the next hour, two more trucks arrived. They positioned themselves on three sides of the canyon to contain the fire. The only side that wasn't manned was the one with the steep rocky drop-off, where the fire wasn't likely to travel.

The fire raged for hours, scorching the canyon and ridding it of its trees and foliage. By the time the emergency crew finally subdued it, the cabin lay in smoking ruins. From the look of it, nothing would be salvageable.

A sooty faced Crew ambled up to Matt and clapped his hand on his shoulder. "'S okay, dude. You can have my room next to Harley's, since I won't be needing it much longer."

"We'll see about that." Matt ran a sweaty arm across his face. It came back black. "So what's this I hear about you breaking parole?"

"Got busted for drug possession a couple of years ago. Never did drugs, myself, but I hung out with a few guys who did. I got out on parole and was lucky enough to land this job. Thought my life had taken a turn for the better, but I was wrong. Coming to work here was when the real trouble started."

Bree, who'd walked up in time to overhear his last remark, made a sound of protest. "Oh, Crew! It couldn't have been all that bad working here."

"It wasn't you, Bree." He shook his head in disgust. "It was Cory. He found out about my record and offered to keep it just between me and him. Even offered to be the one to drive me to my parole officer meetings. Having no idea it was his last night here before skipping town, I stupidly remained in the car while he drove me in the opposite direction I was supposed to go to meet my parole officer. Then he held me there in the middle of the desert for hours. By the time he dropped me back off at the ranch, I was his patsy. I could either do what he said, or he'd turn me into my parole officer."

For an answer, Bree threw her arms around him. "We'll see about that," she announced fiercely. "We need you here on the ranch more than the state of Texas needs one more guy in the pen. Right, Matt?" She sent a pleading look in his direction. "We'll just have to find a way to clear his name."

Matt almost laughed, not because anything was funny, but because of the crazy amount of trust she'd put in him in the last few days. *Fix my brother. Clear Crew's name.* All the while opening a new B&B and getting the ranch's finances back on track. *No problem, darling!*

Watching Matt's expression, Crew swiftly disengaged himself from her embrace. "It's alright, Bree. I've been in trouble up to my eyeballs ever since your dad died." Then he caught himself and looked away guiltily.

"That's not the first time you've brought up the subject of Pops Anderson," Matt noted quietly. "Mind telling us why?"

Crew threw up his hands. "Why not? Doesn't matter anymore. Though I never met 'em, Pops was my uncle."

He went on to briefly share a strange and convoluted story about how his mother married Pops' younger brother but left him without telling him she was pregnant. Right before she passed, she finally admitted the truth to her son about his identity, but it was too late. Both his father and his uncle were gone. He didn't figure Brody or Bree would welcome the addition of a long-lost cousin in their lives right after losing their parents, especially one with a jail record. So he'd kept quiet and worked hard, hoping someday he might be able to share the truth about who he was.

"Welcome to the family." Bree's tone was adamant.

"I second that." Brody, who'd arrived on the scene a few minutes earlier, extended a hand to Crew.

When Officer Emmitt McCarty drove to the ranch, blue lights flashing, to take everyone's statements, Brody filed a number of charges against the absent Cory Brooks. It was only a matter of time before he was located and brought in for questioning.

Then Matt and Brody accompanied Crew to the police station to see what they could do, if anything, to bring him home. For good.

CHAPTER 8: BETTER DAYS

Matt

It took the rest of the evening to sort things out at the police station, with lots of strings being pulled on the part of Emmitt and his associates. In the end, Crew was issued a temporary injunction barring his immediate arrest for violating his parole, and he was remanded into Matt's custody to participate in a newly authorized work release program at the ranch. A hearing was set a month away to review Crew's case and make a final determination on whether or not he'd be returning to jail.

A very tired, very dirty trio of men returned to the Anderson's ranch in Matt's truck. Despite the summer heat, he drove the entire way with his windows rolled down.

"In case you're wondering why the windows are down," he informed Brody and Crew, trying to keep a straight face, "it's because you stink."

"Either that," Brody drawled, rolling his eyes at

Crew, "or he's too entrenched in his own shtank to smell anything beyond it."

All three of them were a sweaty, sooty mess.

For an answer, Crew lifted his arm to his nose and sniffed. "Sorry to disappoint you, boss man, but I think Matt's right. We're rancid."

"Maybe we are, but we're also family, now, something I happen to be pretty happy about." Brody punched him lightly on the shoulder. "So do me a favor and drop the boss man stuff, will you?" He waggled his brows at Matt. "You're more than welcome to transfer the title to him."

"No, thanks," Matt said quickly. "I'm just Matt." Bree's Matt, to be precise, but that wasn't public knowledge yet.

"Well, what am I supposed to call you then, bro?" Crew wrinkled his forehead at his cousin.

"How about keeping things simple and going with Brody?"

In the moonlight, Crew's blue gaze took on a glazed sheen. "I've got family now, huh?"

"Yep." Brody's tone was matter-of-fact. "And since the fire has left me short a set of sleeping quarters for my ranch manager, that means you'll be bunking over in the main house for a bit, so Matt can have a place to crash."

"Or I can keep my usual spot and Matt can have whatever room you've got in mind at the Taj Mahal with the big kids."

"No can do," Brody assured with a knowing grin

at Matt. "The thing is, Matt's sorta dating my sister, even though the two of them think they're keeping it a secret from everyone else. I'm giving them their space, so they can keep up appearances."

Matt was so caught off guard that he nearly choked. He hunched over the steering wheel and gave a cough to clear his airways. "Uh, fellows, just for the record, I haven't asked Bree out."

"Yet," Brody supplied with a grin. "And in the absence of anything official, that keeps you solidly in the friend zone. You, on the other hand, are family, Crew. Guess that means you'll be hanging with the big kids, after all."

"You know what?" Crew threw up his hands in defeat. "Anything's better than being sent back to the pen. I appreciate all that you're doing for me. More than I can say. So if you need anything, and I mean anything, I'm your go-to guy. I'm talking extra chores, additional patrols." He ticked the list off on his fingers. "Whatever you need."

"Whatever I need?" Matt shot him a sly glance.

"Whatever you need, man," Crew assured emphatically.

"Good, because I'm way too dirty and tired to go shopping tonight, and I think we're about the same size."

"Sure thing." Crew's smile was pure innocence. "You can borrow my favorite pink fuzzy slippers and everything."

Matt caught Brody's eye. "Didn't you say something earlier about needing the stalls mucked out again tonight?"

"Eh...then again, maybe I'll keep those fuzzy slippers to myself," Crew amended with a snicker. "Got a pair of gray sweats that might be more your style."

Matt nodded. "The mucking might wait 'til morning then."

"Oh, good!" Crew gave an exaggerated sigh of relief as the familiar ranch lights came into view. The veranda was fully lit on three sides, no doubt Bree's doing, and the dusk-to-dawn lights in front of the barn doors were glowing.

Matt had never been so glad to be home.

"Home sweet home," Crew muttered in contentment, giving voice to the sentiment they were all feeling. He leaned back on the seat where he was perched between Matt and Brody, hands folded behind his head. With a loud, gusty yawn, he proceeded to prop his dusty boots, one atop the other, on Matt's dashboard. Then he closed his eyes.

Matt's jaw dropped. *You did not just put your filthy boots on my dash!* Catching Brody's laughing gaze, he mimed his intentions to tackle the snot-head the moment he turned off the motor.

Brody signaled back that they should converge on his cousin at the same time.

Matt nodded and turned off the ignition.

"Crew sandwich!" Brody crowed.

In unison, the two men launched themselves at the cowboy, arms raised for the maximum gasp effect since the three of them were in true need of showers.

Crew's eyes flew open. He tried to duck and failed. "Shoot!" he gasped from somewhere deep in the dog pile. "A little air, please?"

Matt and Brody complied by dragging him from the truck cab and continuing their scuffling on the front lawn.

The door to the ranch banged open, and Bree came flying down the stairs. "Oh, my lands! Is everything okay out here?"

"No problem, a 'tall," Crew sang out. "I think I just about got these big baboons whipped into shape."

With a snarl of faux rage, Matt tackled him again and pinned him to the ground.

After a moment of hesitation, Brody launched himself back into the fray and ended up straddling Crew's legs.

"Say uncle, you little scamp," Matt taunted. "And I might just forget about the way you stuck your filthy clodhoppers on my dash."

"How about a compromise? I say cousin, and you let me live?" Crew wheedled before convulsing with laughter.

"That'll do, brat. That'll do." Brody rolled into a sitting position, dusting the grass from his shirt.

"Omigosh!" Bree folded her arms, looking astounded. "What are you guys? Twelve? You really had me worried for a minute there."

"Sorry about that," Brody soothed. "Just a few cousins letting off steam."

Crew sat up next to him, jaw working with emotion. That was when Matt realized he was a bit more overwhelmed by his change in circumstances than he was letting on.

Bree was observing him from beneath her lashes and must have noticed it, too. "Crew, if you'll come with me, I'll give you the quick and dirty tour of your new accommodations. Brody texted me about the musical chairs and beds thing on the way home, so Nash and Zane are just about finished moving your stuff over. As for you, Matt," she turned her attention to him, "I took the liberty of taking up a collection, so I could throw an overnight bag together for you. It's sitting on the back porch." The look she gave him made him wish he was much cleaner and that it was just the two of them there on the front lawn.

He nodded, hardly trusting himself to say more. Why had he ever thought she was too skinny or too anything? She looked a million shades of perfect to him, standing there in the moonlight in a white t-shirt and jean shorts with her boots still on. *My country cowgirl.* Clothes-hoarding, makeup-painting supermodels were way over-rated. Bree could throw on a pair of freaking cutoffs and make them look hotter than hot without a single spritz of hairspray or any other product.

Crew leaned in his direction as he curled his long,

lanky frame to his feet. "You got drool on your chin, dude." Then he followed Bree inside, laughing.

As it turned out, the cabin that the ranch hands shared was configured a lot like the one that had burned. Instead of merely two bedrooms sharing a bath on one side of the common area, however, there were an additional two bedrooms on the other side that also shared a bath. In a lot of ways, it reminded Matt of life in the barracks, except better.

Instead of the faded plaid furniture in the hunting cabin, the Andersons had installed a comfy leather sofa in front of a mounted big screen TV in the living room that the ranch hands shared. Flanking the sofa was an additional pair of leather recliners, and anchoring an enormous deerskin rug in the center of the room was a tree trunk coffee table. Matt could see Bree's style of decorating written all over the place.

His room held a double bed with fresh white sheets and four fluffy pillows. A blue and white patchwork quilt was neatly folded and draped like a duvet across the foot of the bed.

Harley knocked on the open doorway to toss him a pile of unfolded towels and washcloths still warm from the dryer. "They're clean," he declared. "You get to do your own folding." He angled his head toward the bathroom they now shared. "I've already cleaned up, so the shower's yours."

Matt gave him a grateful grin. "I can take a hint." Since he hadn't yet unpacked, he carried the overnight bag Bree had packed into the bathroom with him and locked the door. As he stripped out of his filthy gym clothes, he debated between washing them and tossing them. He hadn't been this filthy since the time he'd spent an entire ten days trekking through the Brazilian rainforests on a special mission.

After washing and toweling off, he finally unzipped the overnight bag. He couldn't help smiling at what he saw inside. Apparently, Bree preferred the men in her life dressed like cowboys, because she hadn't bothered to pack any of the usual stuff he wore other than jeans. It was all plaid shirts, boots, and bolos.

No problem, beautiful. He didn't mind dressing like a country boy, so long as she claimed him as hers and only hers.

At the bottom of the bag, he found a note. Well, more like an itinerary. His smile widened as he read it.

> Tomorrow you're mine!
> 7:00 a.m. PT with Brody
> 8:00 a.m. Breakfast (screened-in porch)
> 8:30 a.m. B&B tour and meeting with Brody
> 9:30 a.m. Trip to Amarillo for clothes and supplies (you)
> 12:00 p.m. Lunch at Saltgrass
> 1:30 p.m. — ? More shopping

He could more than handle spending a day with his almost-girlfriend. When he fell into bed, sore and exhausted, he couldn't wait for the sun to come back up so he could get started on their day together.

Ben Taniguchi showed up for their second therapy session via video chat, just like he had the first time, and put Brody through another thorough set of stretches. This time, Brody wasn't quite as pale when they finished.

"When every cell in your body is already sore, you really don't feel the extra pain," he joked.

Ben listened in astonishment as they tag-teamed their way through a recounting of yesterday's fire.

"Shoot, Matt!" he exclaimed when they were through. "I thought you were ditching the military to get *out* of the line of fire."

Matt made a face. "That was the plan, but Texas has turned out to be one wild ride." He went on to share the latest highlights about their barn renovations. "We have a framing crew coming tomorrow to partition off the walls. In another three to five days, you'll be able to step out the actual dimensions of each room."

"That's it. I'm collecting my favor sooner rather than later. Put me down for the ribbon cutting ceremony and grand opening hoopla. I just made up my mind that I'm going to be your first guest."

The note of genuine envy in Ben's voice made Matt wonder if he happened to be on the lookout for another career opportunity. As much of a jokester as he was, though, he tended to keep the details about his private life pretty close to his chest. If he was looking to make a major change like that, he'd tell Matt when he was good and ready and not a second sooner. Regardless, Matt was really looking forward to the visit from one of his favorite military friends.

After another shower, Matt threw on the plaid shirt, jeans, and boots Bree had packed for him. Like Crew, he and Brody were roughly the same height and build, with a few exceptions. Matt was broader in the chest and shoulders. That meant he could shrug the shirt on, but not button it.

With a growl of frustration at not having any clothes that fit on the day he'd be spending with Bree, he stomped his way to Harley's room, hoping to catch the guy around. Unfortunately, he'd already left for breakfast. Feeling guilty about trespassing, but desperate for something to wear, Matt yanked open the older cowboy's top dresser drawer. He intended to make a quick search for a t-shirt and be gone, but what he saw there made him freeze.

After spending a few weeks in Pops' hunting cabin surrounded by dozens of family photos on the walls and shelves, he was very aware of what Pops had looked like. But not once had he seen this particular photo. It was a much younger version of both Pops and Harley. They were holding an enormous bass suspended on a string between them. Scrawled on the back of the photo were a few words: *Family fishing trip. Spring of 1983.*

"Guess you finally figured it out, eh?" Harley's voice rasped from the doorway.

Matt glanced up guiltily, the tails of his shirt flapping over his bare chest. "Sorry for invading your privacy. I needed to borrow a shirt." He waved sheepishly at the open front of his shirt. "So far, nothing Bree scrounged up for me is working."

Harley lifted his dusty Stetson to drag a hand through his silver hair. "I was already toying with the idea of telling you, myself." He gave a dry chuckle. "After what you did for my boy yesterday..." He stopped to clear his throat, his gray-blue eyes going damp.

"You're Pops' younger brother, aren't you?" It was surprising, since both Bree and Brody seemed to be under the impression that he'd passed like Pops.

"Behold the black sheep of the Anderson family." Harley gave a mock bow before clapping his hat back on his head. "I was mad when Dad died and left the ranch to him. Not surprised, mind you. Dad and I never got along, so I wasn't expecting much when he passed. It still stung, though, to be left out of the will completely. Pops, being Pops, offered to deed over that east forty acres to me with the cabin that just burned, but I was young and dumb. Insisted on a cash settlement or nothing, then took off to go live in California. We were estranged for over twenty years." He shook his head. "Saw the notice of his passing in the paper and came to see what became of the place. Boy, was I surprised to find Brody and Bree struggling to run it." He chuckled without mirth. "Doing just about everything wrong possible. Decided right then and there to get myself hired on to help out. Might not ever be able to make things right with Pops, but thought I could ease my conscience a bit by helping his kids."

Matt nodded. "I think everyone would agree you've done that in spades. Things wouldn't be running half as smoothly around here without your mentorship and guidance. The other guys really look up to you."

"Bah!" Harley waved a hand dismissively, as if his contribution was no big deal. "Reckon my kind of input won't be needed much longer. They have you to look up to, now. I see the changes you're making, and they're the right ones."

Matt frowned. "You can't possibly be thinking of moving on. What about your son?" Did Crew even know that he was Harley's son? Since the day he'd arrived to start working for the Anderson's, Matt had considered the incomplete information on their personnel files to be the darndest thing. They were missing the simplest items. Last names, for instance. And now he knew why. A couple of the employees clearly had things to hide, but he intended to change that. Going forward, they were going to foster an atmosphere of transparency, teamwork, and family from top to bottom at the ranch.

Harley shrugged as he considered Matt's question. "Now that Crew has been reunited with his cousins, I reckon he'll be better off without knowing the truth about his old man. Never knew I had a son 'til a year ago when his mother passed. By then, I was too ashamed to admit it."

"From what I understand, your wife took off without telling you. Can't see how that's your fault."

"That's because you don't know how bad of a husband I was. She had her reasons for not telling me, Matt. Good ones. Let's just leave it at that. I've cleaned up my act since then, but some things in life don't come with a redo button, and parenting is one of them. I've already missed out on the first twenty-two years of Crew's life, and—"

"And he ended up in jail, Harley. How has your recent presence in his life done anything but improve it?"

"I don't deserve to be a parent, Matt."

"Are you kidding me?" Matt's face turned red. "Parenting has nothing to do with deserving or not deserving stuff. Take it from a guy who spent ten years in foster care and never got adopted. Family is everything." His chin jutted. "Everything, Harley! There's nothing I wouldn't do to have a father like you in my life. Nothing I wouldn't give. Nothing I wouldn't pay." He was so worked up over the topic, that his voice rose to a near shout. "Crew talks about you all the time, for crying out loud! He thinks the world of you. Sponges up everything you say, brags about everything you teach him. I swear he'd eat dirt if you threw it on a plate and called it steak. That's how much he looks up to you." He broke off his tirade when the first tear trickled down Harley's heavily lined cheek.

The old cowboy ambled across the room and jerked open the third drawer of his dresser. "Take your pick of my shirts, son." He sniffed loudly.

"Thanks." Matt reached for the closest one, a solid navy one. "So you'll stay?" He cleared his throat. "Bree has me running her up to Amarillo today. I wouldn't mind some assurance that you'll be here when I get back."

Harley wiped his shirtsleeve over his eyes. "Not sure why an old feller like me matters so much to a young whippersnapper like you..."

"You matter, Harley. You matter to all of us."

Harley nodded, head still bent, and gave another loud sniff. "Don't reckon I have any other place I'm dying to be."

It also didn't sound like he was all that anxious to be gone. "Good." Relief coursed through Matt's chest. "Can't do it now, but I'd like to sit down with you soon about the new B&B and discuss what everyone's roles are going to be."

Harley snorted. "I'm just an old farmer, Matt, but Crew mentioned something about you grooming him for some big sounding position. Head of maintenance or something."

"He'll be good at it, too."

Harley's head came up, eyes red-rimmed with emotion. "You were serious about it, then?"

"As death and taxes." Matt shrugged out of Brody's plaid long-sleeved shirt to pull on Harley's navy t-shirt. "This is a family business. Only makes sense to have family running it."

Harley gave a jerky nod. "I'll be here when you get back from Amarillo, son."

"Appreciate that." Matt felt a little like weeping, too, as they exchanged a measured look. In his gut, he knew Harley was going to be a man he could count on for a long time to come.

He returned to his room to grab his wallet, phone, and keys. But before he left, he did something he didn't do often. He dropped to a knee by the bed. "Thank you, Lord. For all the things that were meant to be that I couldn't see until now." For Brody, who felt like a brother. For Harley, who was the closest thing to a father he'd ever had. For Crew, who was as annoying as a younger sibling but a whole lot of fun to be around. And for Bree. He was especially thankful for Bree. She was the missing piece of his heart, his compass pointing him true north. A woman he'd met by the most random of chances, whom he'd been falling for ever since.

She wasn't tall and anemic like his supermodel ex. She didn't possess Barbie doll curves or wear the most expensive clothes. Some days she didn't even bother putting on makeup, but she was still insanely beautiful when she was sporting the all-natural look.

He wanted her in his life and at his side more than he wanted financial success. He needed her sass and sweetness as much as he needed the air he breathed.

Who have I been trying to kid? He stood and stretched. Maybe he and Bree were right to wait on officially dating, but there was no such thing as timing the point in which a person fell in love. *I'm already in love with her.* Already in love and already planning to do everything in his power to convince her to take a chance on a real relationship with him.

When he headed over to the ranch house, she was waiting for him on the back porch, impatiently tapping the toe of her boot against the floor. "You're late." She eyed the addition of Harley's blue t-shirt beneath Brody's plaid one.

He shrugged. "Unless you wanted me shirtless while driving you to town..." He took a seat next to her on the porch swing. Pulling the ends of the shirt as close together as they would go, he demonstrated that they remained a good two inches or so away from snapping distance.

"So I misjudged a borrowed outfit, because my boyfriend is more ripped than I realized." She tossed a handful of strawberry-blonde hair over her shoulder, looking anything but displeased. "Somehow that discovery is not breaking my heart."

She was back in her white babydoll dress he thought was so pretty. The one with the tiny red rosettes all over it.

"Is that what I am?" He leaned closer to give the coffee mug in her hand a hungry sniff. "Your boyfriend?"

"I know we talked about waiting about making things official." She yielded her mug to him, and he took a very satisfying swig of it. He tasted almonds, milk, chocolate, and a hint of Bree's lip gloss. It was like skipping breakfast and going straight for dessert.

"But then I realized we were heading into town and likely to run into friends. And I'd have to deal with all that speculation afterward about whether or not you and I are a thing." She shot him a flirty smile that made his heart pound. "Then there's the whole inconvenience of having to spend the day dragging dozens of women off you by their hair after they go all ga-ga over your hot self."

"Dozens, huh?" He'd never had trouble getting a date, but he couldn't recall even one instance in which he'd ever had that many women thronging him.

"At least." She gave a mock yawn. "I'm tired just thinking about it." She abruptly turned to clasp her hands atop his shoulder and rest her chin on them, bringing their faces breathtakingly close. "Wouldn't it be easier to just call ourselves an item and be done with it?"

"Yes!" He reached behind them to set her coffee

mug on the windowsill. Then he turned his head to claim her lips.

His heart raced at the way her lips trembled against his. He liked the fact that he had that effect on her.

"Only you, baby," he declared huskily between kisses. "You're the one for me."

She made a soft, utterly feminine sound of happiness as she wound her arms around his neck. "The truth is, I've been yours since the moment you crashed into my life, Matt. Not sure why I fought it so hard. To borrow one of Brody's favorite sayings, you and I are just meant to be."

Yeah, we are. "I love you, Bree." He rested his forehead against hers, just breathing her in. *You make me happy, baby.* Happier than he'd ever been. With her, he was no longer alone. He finally had a family. He finally belonged.

"I love you, too, Matt. So much that it scares me sometimes."

"There's nothing to be afraid of, baby." He leaned in to kiss her again, very slowly and very tenderly this time.

"I don't want to ever lose you," she whispered.

He knew she wasn't referring to petty, shallow things like cheating. She was referring to the pain of having those she'd loved taken away by circumstances out of her control.

"I plan on sticking around for a long time." He

gazed deeply into her eyes. "A very lo-o-o-ong time."
Until I see my last sunrise and draw my last breath.

"I like the sound of that." She pressed her cheek to his, arms still wrapped tightly around his neck. "You've become very important to me, Matt. So special. So...necessary." The shiver she gave had nothing to do with the temperature. It reverberated all the way to the deepest parts of him.

He cuddled her closer, not ever wanting to let her go. There were so many emotions drenching and running down him that he felt dazed trying to absorb them all. *Bree Anderson is mine. All mine.*

Most unfortunately, there were others expecting him and her to do things besides sit on the porch all day. "Brody's probably waiting for us to do that walk-though with him in the barn." He spoke quietly against her ear, then pressed a few tiny kisses to her earlobe and a few more on the soft skin beneath it.

"Probably." She giggled. "He's pretty punctual."

"I used to be," Matt grumbled, turning his head to kiss his way back across her cheek. He paused to nuzzle the corner of her mouth. "But I have this new girlfriend who's always distracting me."

"What? Like this?" She playfully nipped his lower lip.

Oh, yeah! "Exactly like that." He swooped in for another very thorough, very satisfying kiss that made them several minutes late to their appointment with her brother.

CHAPTER 9: BEST LAID PLANS

Bree

Four months later

Because of how loyal their family and friends were, and how hard working their ranch staff was, and because of how many people came to pitch in and help out (sometimes for nothing more than a free dinner by Bree), the Anderson's barn renovation was completed in record time.

After much debate among their growing family — Brody, Bree, Crew, Harley, and Matt, whom they all considered to be an honorary Anderson — they decided to keep the name of the B&B the same as the rest of their business. And so Anderson Ranch, with its big blue A against a silver star, went on business cards, postcards, flyers, trifold brochures, yard signs, and posters.

Bree took the lead in planning their grand opening celebration. She wanted it to be something big and splashy with a holiday flair since it was December. An event that would draw a crowd with standing room only. One that would be talked about afterward for days, weeks, and months. The word-of-mouth buzz it would create was essential to their launch strategy.

She hummed as she pulled two London broil platters, plus a brisket, from her brand spanking new commercial ovens. It was so much easier cooking in a larger, upgraded kitchen that she did most of her meal prep at the B&B now. Her family and staff sure didn't mind. She could whip up dishes and desserts twice as quickly as before, since she had the capacity to prepare so many different things at the same time.

"Figured I would find you here." Matt's voice drifted her way from the door she'd left propped open.

"It's no secret." She tossed him a happy smile. "This is my new favorite place in the world."

As he strode her way, she twisted off a sample from the end of the brisket and left it sitting there on the serving prongs. His arms came around her, and she added, "Second only to this spot." *In your arms.*

He lifted her feet from the floor and gave her a twirl as he kissed her. "My favorite place is wherever you are, baby."

The moment he raised his head and set her back on her feet, she reached for the sample of brisket. "Want to taste-test something for me?"

"You have to ask?"

She popped the sample in his mouth and waited expectantly while he chewed.

"It's amazing."

She pretended to pout. "You say that about everything I cook."

"Because it's true. Your cooking is amazing. Your kisses are amazing. You're amazing." He cuddled her closer, swooping in to kiss the side of her neck.

"Seriously, though, Matt. If you could change or add one thing about this recipe, what would it be?"

"Hot sauce," he answered without hesitation. "You know I like my food hot and spicy, babe."

"Right." *Ugh!* Those Hispanic taste buds of his. She made a face at him. "I'm not sure how you can taste anything I cook after you drown it in hot sauce."

"See? Now I'm in trouble." He kissed the tip of her nose. "You should've let it go at amazing."

"Not a chance," she scoffed, reaching around the back of his neck to tug a strand of hair. "Never gonna let you go, cowboy." She felt him catch his breath as she stood on her tiptoes to touch her mouth to his.

This was how it always was between them. They scrapped and traded non-stop insults, but their kisses were a desperate sort of cherishing, like they were afraid it might all go away if they so much as blinked.

Then there was the way Matt always kissed her silly that made it impossible to keep thinking at all. Or worrying. Or being aware of anything else that was going on around them, other than his wildly sweet kisses.

When she finally tipped her head back to gaze dizzily up at him, he declared in a low voice, "Never gonna let you let me go, babe."

Someone cleared his throat loudly from across the room. "You'd think all that slobbering in the kitchen would be a violation of health codes or something."

As Matt spun Bree around to face the smirk Crew always seemed to be wearing, for the millionth time she wondered how she'd failed to guess that he was related to her. He looked so much like Harley and Pops that it made her heart ache to look at him sometimes. But her heart never ached for long. Crew always ended up saying something ridiculous that made her feel like laughing.

Today was no exception. She couldn't be happier at the discovery that Crew and Harley were not only related to each other, but also to her and Brody. In every way that counted, thanks to their adoption paperwork. They were family. Her family.

"You bored, Crew?" Matt drawled as he traced a lazy circle on the side of Bree's neck with the hand he still had slung across her shoulder. "'Cause I got a whole list of things that still need to be done before the grand opening."

It was to take place a week from tomorrow.

"Me? Bored? Not even a little." Crew folded his arms and settled back against the door jamb, all six-feet two inches of dusty, rugged cowboy. "What with the kind of show you two are always putting on..." He waved a hand, as if encouraging them to continue.

Gosh, but Crew was way too good looking for his own good! She accepted his unspoken offer for a visual dual and attempted to stare him down without breaking into a smile. With the way his brows dipped down a little in the center, it gave him a naturally broody appearance that was going to attract no small amount of attention from the ladies at the upcoming hoe down. The kind of attention he probably didn't need while trying to get his life straightened out. Good thing he had a cousin like her to help look after him.

"That's it, joker. Get back to work." Matt reluctantly dropped his arm from Bree and stepped away, silently kissing her goodbye with his eyes. "Grab a ladder and a toolbox. We need to adjust those lights on the stage."

"Coming right up, just as soon as I..." Crew flattened himself against the doorway to make room for Matt's broad shoulders to squeeze past him.

Bree shook her head at her cousin, knowing it would have been a lot easier for him to just move out of the way. But no-o-o! That would've been far too easy. He'd much rather continue his endless needling of the guy in charge. Her man.

She was so busy daydreaming about the breadth of Matt's dreamy shoulders and chest that she initially missed the fact that Crew was sidling closer, *much* closer, to the pan of brisket.

"Don't even think about it," she threatened, teeth bared, as he reached for the same corner of brisket from which she'd forked a sample for Matt.

"Too late." Though he drew his hand back, he was already chewing. The brat had stolen his first bite, which meant she'd only caught him reaching for his second one.

"Crew Anderson!" she trilled, advancing on him. She snatched up the serving fork as she passed by the tray of meat in question and brandished it at him.

"Hey!" He shook his head as he backed away from her, hands upraised. "It's your fault for making the place smell so good. A guy can't concentrate on getting any work done out there when you've got the kitchen door propped open like that."

Still scowling at him, she decided to salvage the situation by cross-examining her sly and sneaky would-be taste-tester.

"Is it good?" she demanded.

"Is the sky blue?" he shot back.

"If you could change one thing about it, what would it be?"

"A tad less garlic. Don't take it all out, though. And swap out the brown sugar for honey. Or molasses. Maybe ask Brody. He's always experimenting with stuff out in the greenhouses."

She paused in astonishment at the realization he possessed some seriously discerning tastebuds. "You're right about the sugar." And the garlic. It wasn't too much, though. It was the same amount she always used, but she'd taken a shortcut due to being in a hurry and substituted garlic powder for the fresh-crushed kind. An easy fix on the next brisket.

"No problem." Crew winked. "Trust me. You're not the first woman who's complimented me on my impeccable tastes."

"Do what?" She blinked at him, already mentally retooling the recipe for her homemade marinade.

"Fortunately, there are so many ways to thank a guy for his help. One of your gorgeous smiles. Another sample of brisket…" He cast a longing look at the tray.

"Shoo!" She motioned him out the door with both hands. "If you keep sneaking food, the other guys will go on strike for unfair working conditions."

"Just one more bite," he pleaded, clasping his hands beneath his chin.

"In about another forty-five more minutes, you'll get it," she promised, giving his shoulders a light shove across the threshold. She quickly shut the door behind him.

Her next thought had her swinging the door right back open.

Crew twirled in her direction, a look of hope plastered across his face.

She stepped around him, completely ignoring him. "Matt!" she called urgently, squinting at the stage in search of him.

He was already high on a ladder, tinkering with the stage lights.

"Whatcha need, babe?" He ducked his head below the fixtures to meet her anxious gaze.

"I almost forgot to tell you. That DJ from Amarillo just cancelled on us. Apparently his wife is expecting, and there's some sort of complication going on with her pregnancy. I didn't get the full story, but..." Though her heart went out to the guy, his wife's medical concerns had left her without music for their grand opening festivities. "Do you have any idea who to call next?" She scowled at Crew when he tweaked her braid as he strode past. "And by ideas, I mean somebody cheap. Or somebody who owes us a favor and can do the music for free." They were on a tight budget. Even with Matt's generous six-figure investment in the ranch, there were no extra funds to spare. As a result, they were cutting every corner they could, making do if they couldn't make it themselves.

Matt thoughtfully scratched his chin. "If you want free, we could throw a pink tutu on Crew and toss him on stage."

"Huh-uh." She shook her head emphatically. "I want something that'll make our guests want to stay longer, not run them off."

"Hey, now!" Crew leaped on the stage instead of taking the stairs and broke into a two-step. "You say that like you've never seen me in a tutu."

"Actually, I might know someone who'd be willing to help us out." For reasons she didn't understand,

Matt's smile disappeared. "Can we talk about this?" He nodded in Crew's direction. "In private?"

Crew snorted. "If that's code for more of what I stumbled on in the kitchen, you might as well give up the ladder, dude. I'll handle the stage lights, while y'all go talk *business*." He used his fingers to form air quotes around the word "business."

Matt wordlessly swung down and angled his head at Bree to follow him backstage. But, unlike Crew's humorous prediction, he didn't immediately take her in his arms.

"Well, spill it," she cried. She loved the man to pieces, but she didn't have all day. There were the mashed potatoes to finish mixing and one more brisket to take from the oven before the staff descended on the dining area, clamoring for lunch.

"He's an up-and-coming singer by the name of Gabe Romero. We haven't spoken in ten years. Not since the day he ran away from foster care."

"Gabe Romero," she repeated carefully. Same name. Same foster home. "You mean you have a brother?" she gasped. As in family? He had a freaking family that he hadn't bothered to mention?

"Half-brother," he sighed, scrubbing a hand across the lower half of his face. "Like everything else about my past, it's complicated."

"So you have a brother," she repeated in wonder. It threw her a little off balance, but in a good way. First Harley and Crew, and now Gabe. A few months ago, she thought Brody was all she had left in the world, and now her family just kept growing. It was a little insane, but she welcomed the changes in her life, every last one of them.

"I have a brother," Matt echoed, looking uncertain. "Listen, Bree, I honestly don't know what he'll say if we try to make contact with him." He dug in the pocket of his jeans and pulled out a folded slip of paper. "I've sorta been stalking him online for a while, trying to decide when would be a good time..." His voice faded uncertainly.

Greedy for any information about his brother, she snatched up the slip of paper and hastily unfolded it. It was a news story by an online country music site. It was titled, "Looking for the next big thing in country music?"

"Not just any old singer," she murmured in amazement, "but a really good one."

"Sounds like."

She glanced up in excitement at the possibilities. Contacting Gabe would open the door to having a live singer instead of a DJ at the grand opening, not to mention someone who was family. "Have you ever heard him sing?"

He nodded. "Years ago. And then he stopped."

Her heart ached at the pain she read in Matt's features. For so many teens, foster care felt like the end of the road. No more family. No more home. No one who particularly cared whether you live or died. You were just another statistic buried in a vast, unfeeling system where all the children who weren't wanted got stuck by a society that didn't know what else to do with them.

"Would you like me to be the one to reach out to him?" she offered softly.

"Yeah. That would be nice."

"Hey. I've got this, okay?" She refolded the piece of paper and tucked it in the pocket of the apron she had tied over her jeans. Then she reached up to cup his face in her hands.

"Thanks, baby." He gazed at her, allowing her a rare glimpse at the raw and vulnerable side of him. Most of the world only got to see the tough Ranger, but Matt had finally let her in.

"He's going to say yes, so you better get ready for a family reunion." There was no way she was taking no for an answer from his brother. Now that she knew he existed, Gabe Romero *would* be at their grand opening ceremony. She would move heaven and hell to make it happen, if that's what it took.

Matt nodded, throat working as he swallowed. "It's been so long," he muttered roughly. "Didn't think I needed anyone anymore. Then I met you, and..." He stopped to clear his throat. "I want a family. I want it all."

She stretched to touch her lips to his. "Then let's go get it," she cried.

"I love you so much, Bree." His voice broke as he wrapped his arms around her.

"I know you do." She snuggled closer and scrambled for the right words to lighten the mood. "Because I'm sweet and adorable and—"

"Liar! Liar! Pants on fire."

For the second time in the space of a half hour, Matt and Bree spun around to face Crew.

"Do you have *anything* else to do besides bother us?" Matt exclaimed in exasperation.

"I'm hungry." His mouth quirked in an expression that Bree imagined was an attempt to look pitiful.

"Grow up, already." She rolled her eyes at him. "Can't you see we were trying to have a moment here?"

"I can assure you there will be no growing up here or anywhere else unless you feed me."

"You are unbelievable." She reluctantly slipped from Matt's arms. "Tell you what. Since you insist on staying underfoot like a stray cat, you just got nominated to set the table."

"Aye, aye, Cap'n!" There was nothing but eagerness in his voice and stance as he followed her back to the kitchen.

All joking aside, she welcomed his help. Crew was one of those get-er-done kinda guys. Anything anyone asked of him, he did. Not quietly or without complaint. Not without an exhaustive number of wisecracks and pithy commentary about everything under the sun. Nonetheless, he was a hard worker.

With his assistance, the plates practically took wings and flew to the long bar seating area at the far end of the kitchen. Ever since the renovations had been completed, the staff had been congregating there for their meals.

Interestingly enough, Matt had added the bar feature into the floor plan as a last minute request from Bree, when she decided there just might be an opportunity to hold some sort of couples' culinary class or baking challenge or something at some point. One never knew what all this B&B business could morph into. It was best to keep their options wide open.

Instead of joining the men, Bree slipped away to the tiny office off the side of the kitchen that Matt had insisted on constructing for her. At first she'd thought it was an unnecessary expense; but, sure enough, she'd put the small eight-by-eight space to good use. She did all of her meal planning at her desk there, maintained an electronic inventory of all the kitchen supplies, and had dozens of recipe books lining the walls above her head. Matt had even installed her own powder room through a connecting door, complete with a cozy shower stall and a cabinet with drawers beneath the sink. According to him, she might need a quick cleanup after a major cooking project. It hadn't happened yet, but he'd seriously thought of everything.

Well, now was her chance to pay him back for being so wonderful to her. There was no quick or easy way to get ahold of his brother. No doubt Gabe Romero was strapped to the gills with agents, bodyguards, and the like. So she booted up her computer, instead, and went online to one of his social media sites. As expected, it wasn't accepting posts from strangers like her, but it was still accepting comments on its latest official post — one notifying the world that he was pulling a week-long gig in Dallas. *Starting today?* A closer scan of his performance schedule showed he was booked for seven straight evening performances, Saturday night through Friday night. A mid-December concert with a Christmas theme.

Fortunately, the grand opening of the Anderson Ranch B&B would be taking place at eleven o'clock the following Saturday morning. Her heart raced in excitement. This could work!

She uploaded a photo of Matt in the comments section and captioned it: *Your biggest fan. —Matt*

Then she waited. And waited. And drummed her fingers on her desk and waited some more. Ten minutes clicked past. Then fifteen. Just as she was about to conclude that her brainstorm wasn't working, a private message pinged as it arrived to her inbox.

Call me! A ten digit number followed.

A mixture of excitement and dread coursed through Bree as she dialed. Her call was answered on the first ring.

"Matt?" a man's voice cried hoarsely. "Is it really you?"

Knowing it had to be his brother on the other end of the line, she blinked back happy tears. "I'm his girlfriend, Bree Anderson, calling from Anderson

Ranch up near Hereford. Matt has been wanting to contact you for some time, but wasn't sure if you'd want to hear from him." She paused uncertainly, not knowing what else to say. All the things she'd planned in her head sort of flew out the window now that she had Gabe on the phone.

Silence stretched for so long that she almost wondered if he'd hung up on her. Then he started speaking in a choked voice. "Tell him I want to see him. I want to see my brother."

They spent a full twenty minutes on the phone, exchanging numbers and addresses and making arrangements for him to travel into town to serve as their first guest at the B&B. Or second guest, assuming Ben Taniguchi was still coming.

She could hear the excitement in Gabe's voice grow as they worked through their plan. "Do me a favor, Bree, and sort of play it off like you're working on getting me into town or something. Nothing definite. You're trying. My agent's trying. Everyone's trying to make this work, but blah, blah, blah. Think you can do that for me?"

"Okay." She gave a surprised chuckle, not sure where he was going with this. "If that's what you want." So long as he made it into town, she wasn't going to be too picky about the details.

"I know this was his idea, but I'd like to try to surprise him, anyway."

"That's pretty awesome, actually."

"Should've done this a long time ago," he

muttered in a regretful voice. "Just felt so guilty about abandoning him like that. Heard he went into the military. Tried to look him up a few times, but he was always in training or gone on deployments. Then I told myself if he'd wanted anything to do with me, he would've made it clear a long time ago."

"Actually, he's as nervous as you are about this," Bree confided softly. "If I hadn't offered to be the one to reach out to you, who knows?" Sadly, he might not have ever worked up the courage.

"I'll be there," Gabe assured emphatically. "How many songs do you want?"

"Two or three, maybe. Or whatever you have time for," she added hastily, not wanting to sound too demanding. "We'll start at eleven and end at two. There will be the ribbon cutting and some preliminary festivities, a big steak lunch, then we'll open the dance floor."

"Cool. How about you just consider the music portion of your event covered?" The way he said it made her press a hand to her chest in relief. Didn't sound like he was planning on sending them a big fat bill afterward. He rattled off a few more questions about sound systems and lighting, which she answered as best she could. She promised to double-check with Harley and Crew on a few details and text him any updates.

It was with a dreamy sigh that Bree finally disconnected the line. After what felt like a lifetime of heartache, things were finally going good. All the wrongs in her world were finally being made right.

She frowned as movement outside her office window caught her eye. Standing to get a better look, she held a hand over her eyes to shield it from the sun. Her blood chilled at the knowledge that someone was inside one of the greenhouses. Since her entire staff was seated for lunch, that shouldn't be the case.

Her heart thudded sickeningly as a dozen possibilities sprang to mind, and none of them good. Was it Cory and his cronies at work, stealing from their ranch again?

Over my dead body! Nearly overcome with fury, she bent to unlock her lower desk drawer. Reaching inside, her hand closed around the pistol she kept there. But before she could lift it from the drawer, something hard and cold was pressed to her temple. Something metal.

"Don't do it, Bree." Cory Brooks' hateful voice grated around her. "Just lift those pretty hands of yours, nice and slow, sugar. No sudden moves, or else."

Sugar? How dare he call her that after everything he'd done to hurt her and her family.

"What do you want, Cory?" Her voice was drenched in frost. If her feelings at being in his presence again could transform the room, they'd be standing on a glacier.

"The patent, Bree. Only the patent. Hand it over, and I'll let you live."

She shivered at the mad tenor in his voice, fairly certain that stealing a patent wasn't going to be easy. Weren't copies of that stuff kept on file with the government? "I have no idea what you're talking about," she lied. "All I have in here is recipe books."

"Then you're gonna have to go ask that crippled brother of yours for it. He'll know exactly what you're talking about." He jammed the butt of his pistol more firmly against her head for emphasis.

"Okay." She sucked in a breath. "You're the guy with the gun. I'm assuming that means I can't simply walk out of here and go ask my brother for it."

"Call 'em." He gestured at her phone lying on the desk in front of her. "Tell him to bring you the patent, but don't say why or who's asking for it."

Her heart sank, knowing Cory was lying about letting her live. There was no way he was going to allow her and her brother to walk away from this. They'd accidentally allowed a predator into their lives, and this was the price they would pay for their mistake.

So much for her assumption that things were finally going better for them! They were about to lose everything. For good this time.

Her fingers were shaking so badly that it was difficult to dial her brother.

"Oh, and put it on speaker phone," Cory added while it rang. "That way you won't be tempted to—"

"Hey, there, sis." Brody's affectionate voice filled the room, making her want to weep in despair.

"Uh, Brody?" She had no idea how to alert him to the fact that their lives were in danger without arousing Cory's suspicions, but she had to try. She was probably only going to get one shot at doing so. "Something has come up with my plans for the grand opening ceremonies that's going to require me to take a quick look at your patent."

"Really?"

"Yeah. Please don't ask. It's kind of a surprise, and you know how I adore surprises." She hated them, and he knew it. Hopefully that would signal to him that something was off about her request.

"Where are you?"

"In my office."

"Not gonna lie. That's a weird request, especially coming from you, Miss Allergic-To-Paperwork." He gave a wry chuckle. "But okay. Just give me five to grab it from the safe."

"Works for me." She blinked. They didn't own a safe. *Please let this be your way of telling me you understood my warning.*

Cory reached around her to disconnect the line. "You did good, sugar." He trailed a hand across her shoulder and drew aside her braid.

She squeezed her eyes shut against the rush of revulsion, but this was no time for weeping or fainting. She needed to buy as much time as possible for Brody to do whatever he was going to do.

So instead of slapping Cory's hand away like she wanted to, she faked a sob. "What happened to us, Cory?" She sniffled. "Why did you leave me?"

She knew why, of course. He'd been misappropriating and embezzling funds right and left, all but draining the ranch accounts. He'd left when the money was gone.

"Poor Bree," he crooned. "Always so needy."

Needy! Anger flared through her, heating her insides to inferno levels. Stupid, maybe, to trust a guy like him, but needy was stretching it.

"You're right," she quavered. "I needed you. I still do."

"Aw, sugar." He caressed her cheek. "I'm as sorry as you are that things didn't work out between us. If I thought I stood a chance of…" He bit off whatever he was about to say. "But you were always so loyal to that poor hobbling mess of a brother. More farmer than cowboy. More dirt than brawn."

"More clever than stupid," Brody's voice rang out overhead.

Cory's hand left her cheek. But before he could raise his gun, something slammed into him, knocking him away from her and taking him all the way to the floor.

She whirled in shock to see two men on the floor. Matt was the one on top. His fists were a blur as they slammed into Cory again and again.

Then Brody lowered himself through the ceiling

tile he'd pulled aside, hung there for a moment, biceps bulging, and let go.

He landed on his feet without the help of his cane, a detail Bree's dizzy brain could make no immediate sense of.

Then he was leaning over Matt, pulling him off of their would-be patent thief.

"It's over, Matt. I think he's out cold."

Matt had drawn back his fist again, but Brody shoved it aside. "It's over, man," he repeated. "Emmitt McCarty will be here any minute to make the arrest."

CHAPTER 10: COWGIRLS & CUPCAKES

Bree

The day of the grand opening dawned with a light frost that turned the ranch grounds into a postcard. Plus, there was a chill in the air that made Bree's decorations seem all that more perfect for the occasion.

The big spruce on the front lawn was glistening with white bulbs that they'd opted to leave on for the day. Ornamental pines in urns were artistically arranged on either side of the double glass doors leading inside the barn B&B, and a big Christmas wreath was mounted over what used to be the entrance to the lofts on the second story. It had since been turned into a balcony for the guests who would be staying in the suites on the second floor.

It was absolutely beautiful outside, with just enough frost to cover the once scorched side of the canyon. Cattle bayed in the distance, and a chicken clucked. Inside the barn, however, was where the real magic would be taking place today. It had taken all of Crew's powers of distraction to keep Matt occupied when Gabe Romero's massive tour bus arrived to unload his band and equipment. And it had taken a pretended illness on Harley's part to keep him in their cabin quarters long enough for Gabe's driver to pull the bus out of sight inside the white steel barn.

By the time Matt was free to return to the B&B, their guests were starting to arrive, and he was looking a bit harried from the number of things that had "gone wrong" so far. He breezed into the kitchen in search of Bree, and her heart almost melted at the excruciating concern rolling off of him in waves.

Despite his obvious stress level, he looked divine in his brick red button-up shirt, distressed jeans, and new black boots and Stetson she'd insisted all the guys wear today. Though she wasn't thrilled about the fire that had consumed his entire wardrobe, she'd thoroughly enjoyed getting to help him shop to replace it. Not that he didn't fill his favorite comfy t-shirts in a thousand swoony ways, but there were so many other ways for a guy to slay it in jeans. Thanks to her, he now owned an extensive collection of shirts, vests, blazers, hats, belts, and boots to go with those jeans. And the result was so worth it.

"Wow!" She untied her apron, tossed it aside, and walked straight into his embrace. "You look...wow!"

Instead of kissing her, he scowled with worry down at her. "Gave Harley a Tylenol for the headache and told him to sleep it off. I know he hates missing the festivities, but..." He shook his head in self-disgust. "It's my fault for pushing him and everyone else so hard lately."

Bree slid her hands up his chest to wind them around his neck. "Ain't nobody ever made Harley Anderson do anything he didn't want to. You know I'm right. He's probably faking that nap just to get out of having to dress up and join the crowd." Harley was more of a behind-the-scenes kind of guy, preferring to work in solitude.

"Maybe." Matt frowned in consideration, though she could tell her words had calmed him somewhat. "Harley or no Harley, I just wanted to assure you that our opening ceremony is going to be a success."

"Of course it is!" She pressed her hands to his cheeks. "Because we have the best freaking ranch manager in the state of Texas in charge of it."

The wrinkle in the center of his forehead eased a few more degrees as he wrapped his arms tightly around her. "I just want you to be happy, baby. That's all I've ever wanted."

"Me, too, sweetie pie," Crew mimicked in a falsetto as he sailed past them with a silver tray held high over his head. "Everybody's all happy, happy, happy!"

Matt's mouth quirked upward, as he spun her around to observe the goings-on in the kitchen. Both Nash and Zane were there, looking all western heartthrob in their brick red shirts and silver bolos. Gosh, but they were already a raving success with the guests in the main dining area, especially with the ladies. They were probably going to rack in the tips today.

After much debate among the Anderson staff members, they'd opted to save money by not hiring a catering company or extra help for the day. Instead, they were keeping everything in-house. That meant Bree had done all the cooking, much of it in the days leading up to the event. Today was mostly about warming food and creating killer culinary designs on their square ivory plates.

Nash and Zane were seating guests, taking orders, and serving, while Crew was doing his usual dashing around with whatever he was asked to do — the backfill guy and jack-of-all-trades. Brody was backstage making the final arrangements with Gabe and his band. Matt was serving as their master-of-ceremonies and primary host manning the front door.

"Emmitt's giving me a break, in case you're wondering, so I could grab a quick drink and a kiss." Matt spoke against Bree's temple, breathing her in for a moment.

"Not worried about a thing, Matt. I know you have everything under control."

His scowl returned. "What's up with you, anyway? I thought bleeding sunshine was in Brody's wheelhouse, not yours."

"Hey, you said you wanted me to be happy. Well, I *am* happy. Take the win and run with it, soldier. Not everything has to end in a bloody ambush around here."

He grinned at her reference to how he'd nearly beat the stuffing out of her ex a week ago. Cory was behind bars, awaiting trial and hoping to raise bail. But that was a problem that they would face later. Bree wasn't giving that miserable thug any more head space. Today was about their grand opening and nothing else. It was about making a thousand and one of their biggest wishes come true — hers, Brody's, Matt's, and many others.

"And she's back!" Matt swooped down to give her a firm kiss on the mouth. "Just needed a moment with my sassy girl before we get this party rolling. Speaking of which, how's the music coming?" He struck a hand to his forehead. "Shoot! It's been days since I last asked for an update on Gabe's situation. I'm assuming his trip to town isn't happening at this point?"

"Quit worrying." She stood on her tiptoes to smooth out the wrinkle that had reappeared on his forehead. "Like I told you before, I handed the music over to Brody days ago, and all I can tell you is my brother always has Plan A, Plan B, and Plan C through Z."

"True dat." Matt chuckled as his gaze swept her appreciatively from head to toe. "Nice dress, by the way."

"Just trying to keep the boss happy," she shot back. He loved it when she wore dresses. She had on a red sheath this morning with a Santa-esque white fur collar and cuffs. She'd paired it with knee-high black boots.

"It's working." He ran a finger down her cheek.

Bree grabbed his hand and pressed a kiss to it before letting him go. As he strode away, she wilted in relief. *Whew!* That had been a close call about the music stuff.

Crew sailed back into the room with his tray. This time it was full of empty glasses instead of full ones. "You know what? I think I'm going to get my GED and start taking those college classes you talked about," he informed Matt airily.

"Really?" Matt paused his exit march. "What brought about this monumental change? Is bussing tables suddenly too good for you?"

"Nope." Crew tossed him a cocky grin. "Just happen to be a big fan of your idea of management. You know." He waved a hand sarcastically. "Standing around. Kissing your woman all the time."

"Whatever." Matt pushed Crew's hat brim down to his nose and finished making his way out the door.

Crew shoved it back in place and gave Bree an innocent look. "Did I say something wrong? I was just trying to pay the guy a compliment."

She didn't find his crabbing worthy of a response. One more quick spin around the kitchen proved they were ready to begin serving as soon as Matt finished his opening remarks. Chef duties aside, Bree had no intention of missing his big moment, though. Smoothing her hands down the sides of her dress, she made her way from the kitchen. She took her position along the wall in the main dining hall as the lights started to dim.

A spotlight flashed on to illuminate the podium on the left side of the stage. It was positioned in front of the tall black curtains, which remained closed.

Matt jogged up the stairs. "Welcome, friends and family, citizens of Hereford, Canyon, Amarillo, and all the surrounding areas. Thank you for attending the grand opening of the all-new B&B at Anderson Ranch. For those of you who've been lucky enough to snag a sample of Anderson beef in the past, you're in for a real treat today." He went on to thank their biggest donors and contributors. Then he gave the signal for the stage curtains to open. Because of their carefully crafted itinerary, he assumed there'd be a DJ playing background music, while Bree and her staff served the steak lunch. They'd sold tickets in advance to ensure they would start off with a full house, but already the waiting room was filling with more folks who were anxious to be seated.

The stage curtains rolled open, and Gabe Romero was standing there with his band, all decked out in red and green western shirts with plenty of fringe and bling. A few hoots sounded, and a smattering of applause gathered steam as their audience recognized their guest singer and went a little wild. It was at least a full minute before they quieted enough for Brody to join Matt at the podium.

"We have a little surprise for the best ranch manager in the west, because we were lucky enough to reserve Gabe Romero and The Texans for today's musical performance. In case you're wondering why these two cowboys look so much alike, it's because they're brothers. Brothers who haven't seen each other in a long while, thanks to Matt's military duties and Gabe's jam-packed tour schedule. Well, we got our heads together and decided to change that, because Christmas just wouldn't be Christmas without our families, right?"

There were a few cheery whistles and whoops over that comment.

"So without any more ado, let's give it up for Gabe Romero and the Texa-a-a-ans!" Brody sang out.

Gabe's lead guitarist gave a crazy, wonderful entry solo. His drummer joined him, and they crashed through a catchy opening sequence. Then Gabe's familiar country western twang filled the room. Many of the guests joined in when he reached the chorus, several of them tapping out the rhythm with the toes of their boots.

Matt's stunned gaze sought out Bree. She smiled at him over the tops of the white linen-clad tables with their pine bough centerpieces and spice-scented candles. She wasn't sure if he could read her expression from that far away, but she mouthed the words, "I love you!"

In response, he pressed a hand over his heart, dark eyes glinting with emotion. When Gabe finished his opening number, Matt jogged onto the stage and enveloped him in a bear hug. Cameras flashed wildly as several local reporters caught the poignant reunion between the two brothers.

Many eyes were damp and smiles and laughter were spilling freely by the time Bree gave her staff the signal to start the appetizer line. Since it was their opening day, they'd simply sold a per head cover charge. That way they could serve a wide sampling of menu entrees. Today wasn't so much about making money, as it was getting the word out about everything Anderson Ranch had to offer.

There were brochures on each table about the various overnight packages for sale, their restaurant hours, event reservation policies, trail rides, and more.

A quick glance at the reception desk outside the dining area proved that Harley was very much back in the saddle and fully prepared to start taking reservations. There'd never been a lick of anything wrong with his health. He'd just been running interference with Matt to keep their forthcoming surprise about Gabe's arrival intact.

Gabe dialed down the volume and crooned out a slower country song while their guests dug into their food. With respect to their limited staff, Nash and Zane had set up a smorgasbord line against both outer walls, so it was mostly a matter of keeping the warming trays filled and on the proper heat settings while their guests essentially served themselves. As tummies became filled, Crew bussed tables, and Brody escorted guests to the surrounding balcony seats and back out to the waiting area, so that new guests could take their turn at the food lines.

Bree returned to the kitchen to fill another dessert cart. As with the main entrees, she and her team had done all the baking in advance to ensure things would run as smoothly as possible today. After much debate, they'd decided to keep things simple, as in cupcake-sized simple. She'd baked hundreds of oversized cupcakes — vanilla bean, red velvet, milk chocolate, lemon twist, banana nut, coconut cream, and a half-dozen more specialty flavors. She'd drizzled them all with her family-secret glaze that Shanna Anderson had taught her how to make. Perched on the top of each mini-cake was a candied A ranch logo.

Matt joined her to help wheel out the next pair of dessert carts to the ooh's and ah's of their guests waiting in line. They remained by the carts, greeting friends and meeting newcomers.

Star Corrigan gave a squeal of greeting and stepped out of line to throw her arms around Bree. She reminded Bree of a merry Christmas elf with her pixie hair style and pine green sweater. "This is the most amazing place." She gazed around the barn, dark eyes wide with admiration and excitement. They grew a little dazed as they landed on Brody. "Oh, wow! No cane, huh?"

Bree glanced over her shoulder at Matt. "No cane," she agreed happily. "He's been in physical therapy for a few months, and he's a lot better." Brody's improvement in mobility was very much due to the hard work of Matt and his friend, Ben, who she was dying to meet. Last she'd heard, his flight had been delayed due to a snowstorm in Colorado, but he was still trying to make his way there.

"Hmm." Star's lush lips pursed in speculation. "Might have to see if your brother is up for a dance later on."

"You should do that." Bree gave her another quick hug, wondering all over again what had happened between her and Brody. At one point, they'd been high school sweethearts. Never before had Bree met two people more perfect for each other. Then, boom. Brody's accident had disrupted their universe. And afterward, they'd drifted apart. To this day, it still made no sense to Bree, but neither Brody nor Star had been willing to talk about it.

Gabe took the stage again. "Alright, folks! How many of you wore your dancing boots today?" A series of colored lights flashed across the room, illuminating the extra spaces the staff had left for dancing.

Matt knew he and Bree were supposed to be on the clock, but to heck with that! She'd worked so hard to make today happen that she deserved a break. Not to mention he'd most definitely worn his dancing boots. There was no way he was passing up the opportunity to spin his favorite five-star chef, business partner, and best friend around the dance floor.

Gabe launched into a song with a rousing two-step rhythm that quickly brought a good number of guests to their feet. Couples paired off and small groups formed. The dancing even spilled out to the waiting area. After a few more energetic numbers, Gabe motioned for his band to strike up a slower song.

Matt wrapped his arms around Bree and rocked her gently side-to-side. "Thank you." He spoke against her temple, searching for the words to express everything he was feeling. "For bringing my brother into town. For making me happy. For loving me. For being my..." He stopped, stunned at what he'd almost said. *For being my family.*

Because that's who she was. She was why he'd wanted so badly to make Anderson Ranch a success. She was his biggest reason for waking up each morning. She was the love of his life — all of his hopes and dreams poured into one slender woman in cowgirl boots.

He suddenly didn't want to wait any longer to tell her what had been on his heart for days. Unwrapping his arms from her waist, he reached for her hands and sank to his knees in front of her.

A few murmurs around them told them his new posture had been noticed, but he didn't care. This wasn't part of their grand opening ceremony. This was the next big step in their lives that they were finally ready to take.

"I love you, Bree Anderson." He was surprised at how well his voice carried across the dance floor. "You mean everything to me. So much, that I didn't want to go another second without telling you that you're the one. You're the only one for me, and I want you by my side for the rest of my life. Will you marry me?"

Her blue eyes had gone bluer as he spoke, and glossier as they filled with happy tears. Her lips parted on a gasp when he asked her the big, all-important question.

"Yes," she whispered, squeezing his fingers. "Yes," she repeated a little louder, as if fearing he hadn't heard. One diamond-bright tear slid from beneath her lashes and rolled down her cheek.

He stood and swept her into his embrace, claiming her lips. The dance floor erupted into cheers and clapping.

Matt felt the dampness of more tears as he palmed her cheek and kissed her in a way that made it clear to anyone who was watching that he was never, ever going to let her go.

Somewhere in the distance, he heard a familiar scoundrel's voice drawl, "And they're kissing again. Shocker!"

EPILOGUE

Ten months later

June is for weddings. Mine. Bree gazed down at her ivory wedding dress, hoping like crazy she hadn't made the biggest mistake of her life. Now would've been the perfect time to have a mother advising her on her wardrobe. Correction, last month would have been the perfect time — back when she had gotten a wild hair to go dress shopping all by herself.

"I should've taken you with me," she murmured to Star, as she reached up to lightly skim the lace wrapped around her upper arm. It was an off-the shoulder dress with a fitted lace bodice and a long, fluttery asymmetrical skirt. It dipped to her ankles in the back but came up to her knees in the front. Why? So she could wear a pair of blasted cowgirl boots! White ones with heels that she'd specially purchased and never worn before today. But seriously! *Who in the world wears cowgirl boots to their wedding?*

"Taken you where, hon?" Star murmured. She was in a champagne pink dress, designed in a similar style to Bree's dress, except shorter. One pink-lacquered finger was scrolling the screen of her phone. Whatever she read heightened the color in her cheeks and made her suck in a shallow breath.

"Wedding dress shopping!" Bree wailed. For a moment, she wanted to throw open the door to the guest item check-in area, where she and Star were closeted at the front of the B&B and take off running. Anywhere. Away from the crowd of guests waiting for her outside the door. Maybe she should have reserved a church building. Maybe she should have designed a more traditional ceremony with rose trellises and a proper veil, instead of the simple white rosebuds she'd threaded through her unbound hair.

"It wouldn't have made any difference," Star said firmly, pocketing her phone. "You found the perfect dress all on your own." She reached out to straighten the white gold locket that Bree was wearing at her throat. It contained side-by-side photos of Mom and Pops, the closest she could have them to her heart on her wedding day.

"It wasn't even advertised as a wedding dress." Bree lifted the skirt a few inches and dropped it.

"So?" Star waved a hand scoffingly. "It was the right one for you, and Matt is going to love you in it.

He's marrying you, Bree, not some silly dress." She leaned closer to tap her friend's wrist for emphasis. "His strong and sassy cowgirl. His award-winning country chef."

A wry smile curved Bree's lips. "It was only a college-level contest."

"You're the only woman in the world who holds his heart in her hands," Star continued as if she hadn't heard. "And I will totally deny this if you ever try to throw it back at me, but you need to hear it." Her smile turned tremulous. "There is nothing I wouldn't give to trade places with you right now."

Bree peeled out a laugh and pretended to misunderstand. "Sorry, chickadee. Matt's taken."

"Very funny." Star rolled her gorgeous dark eyes. "All I meant was I wish I was lucky enough to be marrying the man I love."

Bree's heart ached for her friend. "Are you ever going to tell me what happened between you and Brody?" she sighed.

"Not on your wedding day." Star reached for Bree's hands. "That's what your sweet mama would say if she were here. Ah, ah, ah!" she warned when Bree's eyes started to glisten. "No tears today. Only happiness. And I've never met a couple who deserves to be happy together more than you two."

"Thank you for being here for me." Bree had no one else of the female persuasion to stand in for her. No other family members. No other close friends.

She was pretty much surrounded by guys most of the time.

"Always, hon. As Lara and Elle like to say, you're our honorary fourth sister, which makes us practically family."

Bree swallowed the stab of envy that accompanied her words. Gosh, how wonderful it must be to have two sisters! *Real* ones, not "practically" or "like" ones. The kind a girl could borrow clothes from, share secrets, and giggle with about boys.

A quick triple-knock sounded outside the door.

"That would be Crew." Star squeezed her hands one last time, then let go.

They stared at each other for a moment before dissolving into giggles.

"Our official wedding coordinator and event planner," Bree snickered. "Gosh, but he's a hoot, isn't he?"

"Your hoot, not mine, thankfully," Star returned in a voice that clearly indicated she thought the man was nothing but trouble. "Okay." She briefly closed her eyes. "Tell me again that this dress is the perfect color for my summer tan, and that I'm totally killing it in these heels."

The only reason Bree could think of that was making her friend so nervous was the fact that Brody would be waiting for her on the other side of the door. "To borrow a few words from a very wise friend, my brother is going to love you in that dress." It was as close as she'd ever come to telling Star that she thought Brody still had feelings for her.

Star's dark eyes snapped open. "Thank you. I really hope you're right." Then she opened the door and allowed the smirking Crew to lead her to Brody's side.

He returned seconds later. "You're up next, boss lady."

She couldn't help smiling. He was that good looking. "You look really great." He, Nash, and Zane had agreed that their uniform of the day would be white button-up shirts, black ties, and gray vests over jeans and boots. A little more polished than usual, while staying in tune with the country western theme of the Anderson Ranch B&B.

"I always look great, Mrs. Almost Romero. You, on the other hand..." He gave a low whistle as he surveyed her, shaking his head. "Let's just say I am never going to get married unless another woman exists who's even half as hot as my favorite cousin." He crooked his arm at her. "Which probably means I'm doomed to remain single until the end of time."

By the time he delivered her to her escort, her tears were long gone. "Thank you, Crew." She leaned in to kiss his cheek. "For everything."

He winked. "What can I say? I'm the world's best git-er-done guy."

"Yes, you are." She blew one more kiss to him before turning to face Harley.

"Our beautiful bride." Harley surveyed her with a fatherly pride that went straight to her lonely heart and nestled there. He was wearing the gray suit, black shirt, and champagne pink corsage that he, Brody, and Matt had agreed upon.

"Thank you for agreeing to walk me down the aisle." Bree momentarily rested her head against her uncle's shoulder. He was the closest thing to a father she had left.

"I couldn't be more honored that you asked me." He held out his arm. "I think I hear the music. That's our cue."

She nodded, no longer trusting herself to speak. It felt like she was sashaying her way through a dream as they slowly made their way down the aisle between their rows of guests.

The B&B dining hall had been transformed into a country wonderland. There were strands of white lights strung overhead, white ribbons tied to the back of each chair, and a white carpet walkway strewn with pink rose petals.

Brody had invited the stooped over minister from the little white church down the road to preside over their ceremony. They'd moved a rustic pine podium to the front of the room for him to stand behind with his Bible. Brody and Star stood on opposite sides of the podium, facing her, and Matt waited for her directly in front of it.

He was dressed the same way as Harley and Brody, with two very distinct exceptions. His corsage was a white rose, and he was wearing a black felt Stetson.

As Star had promised, his gaze lit at the sight of her and continued to glow as Harley transferred her hand from his arm to the arm of her groom-to-be. The way he was looking at her made her feel every shade of wanted and cherished. It was enough, more than enough.

Her fears about her dress evaporated, as she turned with him to face the minister.

"Dearly beloved," the man droned in an old-school, sing-song voice that made her smile. It warmed her heart to know that her adoptive parents had listened to him deliver countless sermons in that same sing-song voice.

The ceremony was short but beautiful. It was full of age-old scriptures, a few doses of wisdom and admonishment, and the kind of promises that were meant to be kept for eternity.

Bree whispered her heartfelt, "I do," while Matt's gaze burned into hers. In only a handful of minutes, she went from a blushing, single woman to a wildly happy, slightly overwhelmed bride.

Matt dipped his head over hers to brush their lips together, adoring her without words. Then he turned with her to their family and friends, where they were showered with smiles, a few happy tears, and more than one sigh of envy.

Instead of the traditional promenade back up the aisle, they'd opted to end the ceremony, hands clasped before their guests, with a final prayer. Then, without any further ado, Bree spun around a few times and tossed her bridal bouquet of white roses and baby's breath into the air.

A collective gasp rose when the bouquet seemed to go straight up and come nearly straight back down. There was only one other woman standing anywhere near it. After a wide-eyed look of sheer amazement, Star reached out at the last minute and caught it.

It was one of those startled reflexes, something she'd probably done simply so that the beautiful blooms didn't have to hit the floor. She blinked a few times at them, and her pink-painted lips parted. Then she flitted the briefest, most furtive look at Brody before shooting a questioning smile at Bree. It held a hint of accusation, as if she was wondering if Bree had tossed the flowers to her on purpose.

Brody was the first to reach Bree. He enclosed her in a bear hug, then lifted her into a quick twirl. She could see the joy shining in his eyes to be able to pull off such a maneuver, now that he was no longer chained to a cane.

"Congratulations, sis. I'm happy for you." He kissed her cheek but couldn't resist sounding like a brother when he added, "Nice throw at the end. It's no wonder your softball career was a one-season wonder."

She hugged him back. "Well, Brody, you're the one who's always telling me that things happen for a reason." She preferred to think that Star was exactly the one who was meant to catch her bouquet.

"Yep. You've said it a good few hundred times to me, too." Matt reached around her to lightly tap his fist to Brody's shoulder. "And you were right."

He lifted Bree's hand bearing his diamond to his mouth to kiss her fingers. It was a big, square-cut gem that flashed each time it caught the sunlight from the tall loft windows.

Gazing deeply into her eyes, he drawled, "I love you, Bree Romero." He pressed her hand to his heart. "Marrying you was most definitely something that was meant to be."

Like this book? Leave a review now!

Join Jo's List and never miss a new release or a great sale on her books.

Want to find out why Brody and Star broke up and why both of them are still secretly hoping for a second chance at happily-ever-after? Keep turning the page for a sneak peek at ***Born In Texas, Book #2: BEST FRIEND HERO*** *right now!*

Can't get enough of Jo's sweet contemporary romance stories? Check out ***HEART LAKE #1: Winds of Change****, coming April, 2021 — when a cowboy bad boy comes face-to-face with the town darling, who stole his heart years ago before she left for college. And now she's back to torment him* *all over again with what might have been if she'd never left Texas in the first place!*

Much love,
Jo

SNEAK PREVIEW: BEST FRIEND HERO

From best friends, to high school sweethearts, to barely talking... He knows he was a fool to let her go, but it's going to take a miracle to convince her to give him a second chance.

Brody Anderson and Star Corrigan made all the superlatives in their high school yearbook, right down to being voted the Most Romantic Couple. But life happened, tragedy struck, and they drifted apart. No, it's actually worse than that. He allowed his pride to push her away.

Now that he's back on his feet after a near-crippling accident and his ranch is finally turning a profit, Brody can't get Star out of his mind. More than anything, he wants her back. But will she be able to trust him again? Will she believe he has what it takes to stand by her and fight for her this time around, no matter what? And can he love her the way she's never stopped hoping and dreaming he will love her someday?

★ ***BORN IN TEXAS** is a series of sweet and inspirational, standalone romantic suspense stories about small town, everyday heroes. **WARNING**: Lots of heart, plenty of humor, and always a happily-ever-after!*

Best Friend Hero
Available in eBook, paperback, and Kindle Unlimited!

Much love,
Jo

SNEAK PREVIEW: WINDS OF CHANGE

Heart Lake

The cowboy bad boy who broke her heart years ago and the career opportunity that offers them a second chance at happily-ever-after...

While they were growing up, Hope Remington was the darling of Heart Lake, and Josh Hawling was...well, bad news. And now she's returning after ten years of being gone, with a PhD and plans to use her new position to transform their struggling high school into a center for educational excellence.

She soon realizes that her biggest challenge isn't going to be the rival gangs embedded in the student body, although they're a close second on the list. It's Josh Hawling, who has somehow convinced their aging superintendent that he and his security firm partner can coach their backwoods collection of farm boys into a football team that'll make the playoffs.

How is a woman of her refined background and education supposed to improve test scores and graduation rates when her students' biggest idol is a man who spent more time in the principal's office than in the classroom? Even though she feels safer having him on their crime-ridden campus, she's so not looking forward to her daily encounters with his cocky self. Or being socked in the heart all over again by his devastating smile. Or having to finally face her unwanted attraction that might have kindled into a lot more if she'd never left Texas in the first place.

Welcome to Heart Lake! A small town teaming with old family rivalries, the rumble of horses' hooves, and folks — on both sides of the law and everywhere in between — that you'll never forget.

HEART LAKE
Winds of Change
Song of Nightingales
Perils of Starlight
Return of Miracles

Heart Lake #1: Winds of Change
Available in eBook, paperback, and Kindle Unlimited!

Much love,
Jo

SNEAK PREVIEW: THE PLUS ONE RESCUE

A lot of people view the life of a soldier as a glorious and honorable thing. In recent months, the social media sites had been overflowing with pictures of the lucky soldiers who got to return home to kiss their wives, husbands, and children.

But for Axel Hammerstone, it had been both a physically and mentally exhausting journey to reach his hometown — one that had taken six months if he counted his stopover in the hospital. In minutes, his plane would land in Dallas, and he couldn't have felt less like celebrating.

Why me? Why did I get to come home? He was just a regular Joe who'd been raised in foster care — no family, no roots. *Shoot!* There were far better men and women than him who were never coming home again. That was the irony of war.

He stared out the window of the Boeing 747 as it circled the Dallas/Fort Worth International Airport. It was overcast with a hint of rain. Decently windy, if the air currents rocking the wings of their plane were any indication. *Makes a poetic sort of sense.* His upper lip curled at how fitting it was for the skies to weep instead of welcome him.

Nine months in the God-forsaken wilderness of Afghanistan, followed by another six months of convalescing at a specialized burn unit in San Antonio, followed by yet a few more weeks of medical out-processing at Fort Sam Houston, and still there was no one coming to greet him for his troubles. No wife and no children. Not even a girlfriend. He had no ties to anyone, actually. His foster parents — who hadn't sent a single letter or care package during his entire tour overseas — had already texted to say they were tied up at some court hearing.

Axel hadn't bothered notifying the family of his best friend, the Zanes, that he was returning home, though they probably would have met him at the airport if he had. He saw no point in adding the sight of him to their overwhelming grief.

He and their only son, Marcus Zane, had played football together in high school, graduated together, and enlisted in the Marines together. Fifteen months ago, they had been deployed to Kandahar together. Axel made the sign of the cross on his chest. *May you rest in peace, brother.* Unfortunately, Marcus wasn't one of the lucky ones. He should have been, but he wasn't.

The plane landed with a bumbling double bounce that made the petite elderly woman sitting to his right gasp and dig into the arm rests with both heavily be-ringed hands. Her skin was so pale that it made her freshly lacquered fingernails look like they were dripping blood. They hadn't exchanged two words the entire hour of their flight, which was fine with Axel. He wasn't in the mood for chatting. However, he noted that she seemed to be having difficulty catching her breath, something a man trained to serve and protect was unable to ignore.

He bent his head a fraction to get a better look at her face. "Are you alright, ma'am?"

Her slightly upturned brown eyes were wide with fear, and her pale skin was crinkled like a hundred folds of paper at the corners. She blinked a few times and slowly raised her face to his. "Did we crash?"

The ludicrous question amused him, but he kept a straight face. "Nah. We just landed with a bit of a bounce. Pilot probably needs a refill on his coffee." They were flying first class, thanks to the automatic upgrade he'd been given when he flashed his military

ID at the ticket counter, so he glanced around for the nearest stewardess. He wondered what the odds were of securing a bottle of water this late in the trip. His companion sure looked like she could use some refreshment.

Her pursed lips relaxed into a hint of a smile. "For a second there, you sounded just like my Kento." She looked like a typical first-class traveler in her black designer pants suit, lacy white blouse, and fat diamond pendant necklace. Her manicure was perfect, as was her makeup. Every silver hair in her French braid up-do was in place. She was clearly of Asian descent.

Axel arched a brow at her. "And he is?"

"The love of my life." She released her white-knuckled grip on the arm rests to sit up more fully in her seat.

He felt a pang of something. Envy? Resentment? *That's just great. I'm jealous of an old lady.* He scrubbed a hand over his jaw, irritated with himself. *My life just hit a new low.* He forced himself to swallow the prickle of bitterness on his tongue. "Guess that means your cowboy will be waiting for you outside the jet ramp." *Lucky you!*

This time she chuckled as she spared him another sideways glance. "I'm actually returning home after paying him a visit. My granddaughter is the one who will be waiting for me."

"Uh, that's nice." Axel sensed a story, but didn't consider it his place to ask questions.

"It is. She puts up a terrible fuss every time I make my annual visit to the Sam Houston National Cemetery."

Ah. Axel's brain froze. Her husband was gone. Just like Marcus was gone, along with way too many of his other Marine buddies. His mind drifted back to that fateful night on the outskirts of Kandahar.

———

"So I met this girl the other night." Marcus nudged Axel with one broad shoulder as they jostled along a dirt road in their armored light utility vehicle. They were standing in the opening in the center of the truck. Axel was serving as their primary lookout, while Marcus manned their mounted .50 caliber machine gun.

"Right." Axel didn't bother muffling a snort. They were deployed, for crying out loud. They had no social life. None whatsoever. Other than the handful of female Marines in their unit and the one female at the last MP checkpoint, there were no women in their lives.

"You talking about the one who frisked us at the MP checkpoint?" Axel shook his head in exasperation. She was attractive in a blonde, beach-babe sort of way. He'd give Marcus that. But she hadn't seemed very interested in their sandy, sweaty platoon. At least not in the romantic way. All she'd done was process them and their equipment through the checkpoint and provide an intel update about the pack of terrorists they were tracking through the surrounding foothills.

Marcus grinned and flexed his upper arms. "What can I say? She liked what she saw."

Axel used his shoulder to shove his friend back. "Gee! What gave it away? Her snarl when you asked for her number?" Marcus was such a player. Ever since their high school football days, he'd been landing dates with the prettiest, most popular girls – from their homecoming queen to the winner of their town beauty pageant. Normally, the guy could charm the skin off a rattlesnake, but the gorgeous military police chick at their last checkpoint had appeared solidly immune to his attempts at flirting with her.

Marcus waggled his black brows, making a trio of wrinkles form in the center of his wide, dark forehead. He pushed his kevlar lower, like one might do to a favorite Stetson, hiding his expression. "That and the fact that she whispered her cell phone number to me when she handed back my ID."

"You're kidding." Axel shook his head at his friend, whose brows remained raised in challenge. "Okay. You're not kidding. Wow! Well, there you go, man, living up to your reputation." He hardly saw the point in flirting with a soldier they'd likely never see again. A thought struck him. "You do realize it's probably an old number." One that wouldn't work when they got back to the States. Most soldiers he knew cancelled their cell phone plans while they were overseas to save the cash.

"Oh, ye of little faith." Marcus ducked his head and lowered his voice, so it wouldn't carry down to their driver. "She promised it'll work when she pops her sim card back in."

Axel shook his head again. "It'll be another three months, at least, before we get out of here." None of their personal electronic devices would work until they were back in U.S. air space.

"So? All I gotta do is remember her number for that long."

"What makes you think she'll even remember you when you call?" *Much less, pick up when the phone rings?* Axel couldn't believe they were having such a mundane conversation about girls and dating on the outskirts of Kandahar. The days of wearing blue jeans and drinking soda seemed so far away here in the craggy foothills of the Sulaiman Range. Fingers of green vegetation streaked down the dusty mountain ridges, though the distant peaks of the Hindu Kush remained capped with white. It was early March, the in-between season in terms of temperature and precipitation.

"Because she's the one."

"If you say so." Axel wasn't buying it. He didn't believe in things like love at first sight. A blur of movement on the other side of the pass captured his attention. Their trio of armored utility vehicles was escorting a much larger Marine convoy through the mountain pass. They were the forward-most eyes and ears.

"I do." Marcus cocked his gloved thumb and forefinger like a hand gun.

"Sounds like you're already practicing your wedding vows," Axel scoffed, whipping out his binoculars for a closer look.

"Practice makes perfect," Marcus quipped, leaning into his scope to follow Axel's line of sight.

A flash of sun hitting glass against the distant mountain ridge was Axel's only warning there was trouble ahead. A sniper, most likely. He slapped his hand on the side of the vehicle to get their driver's attention. "Puppies and kittens about two clicks north," he growled into his shoulder microphone. It was a private joke — his platoon's way of identifying enemy combatants.

The driver immediately halted their vehicle.

"Got 'em marked." Marcus rattled off the coordinates, and Axel swiftly radioed them in. "Two tangos for sure. Maybe three."

Three snipers. Axel's pulse sped in anticipation of the coming encounter. A burst of adrenaline in times like these was good. He always welcomed the way it heightened his senses and helped him focus.

The rogues in the mountains were, if anything, unpredictable in their construction of hodgepodge fortifications. Most times, they were holed up with nothing more than a handful of M-16s. Once in a while, however, they managed to score a grenade launcher. Which meant Axel and his comrades always needed to expect the unexpected...

"Another tango spotted," the lookout in the vehicle directly behind them warned. "Click and a half east."

"Tango spotted south. We're boxed in," the last lookout chimed in breathlessly.

Okay. It was starting to sound like a whole lot of not good. Axel's blood pounded through his veins as he bent over his sniper rifle, took aim, and awaited his captain's orders.

"Charlie mike with extreme prejudice!" Captain Ramos barked across the line. It was a direct order to continue their mission, which was simple — to eradicate the countryside of enemy combatants seeking to unseat the newly installed government.

Axel forced himself to breathe in and out in an even cadence. He would need all his wits about him if they were rolling their way into a bonafide terrorist stronghold. At the very least, his day was about to get a lot more interesting.

"I'll be expecting you to rent a tux when we get home, bro," Marcus said softy as he tightened his finger on the butterfly trigger of his .50 cal.

If their situation had been any less serious, Axel would've laughed. His friend was referring, of course, to their longstanding promise to serve as the best man at each other's weddings. "Don't you need to propose first?"

"A mere technicality." In the next second, the .50 caliber machine gun was belching lead and smoke.

A much larger-than-expected explosion billowed in the distance. Then a series of subsequent explosions worked their way in a half-circle around their trio of armored vehicles.

"What the—?" Marcus lifted his head from his scope.

"It's like we triggered some sort of chain reaction." Axel watched in growing alarm as the explosions circled ever closer to their vehicle. "We have to get out of of here." *Or be roasted alive.*

Unfortunately, there was no driving their way out of this. He hastily scanned the terrain. The northern and southern routes were in flames. The east ended in a fairly steep drop-off, leaving their only way of escape to the west. *Sort of.* It was all mountains — the kind that went straight up. But they were fresh out of options, since it was the only route that wasn't on fire or wouldn't plunge them straight to Kingdom Come.

Trails of fire shot across the path of their vehicle, enveloping them with smoke and making it harder to breathe. Axel instinctively slid his neck warmer over his mouth and nose, knowing they might only have seconds left to evacuate. Once the flames reached the gas tank, it would turn their truck into a bomb.

"Out! Now!" Marcus fumbled with the bolts on his .50 cal.

"Leave it!" Axel shouted. "There's no time." He slapped Marcus's shoulder for emphasis.

He nodded, leaped to the ground and turned around to assist Axel down with his sniper rifle.

"Come on!" Axel jogged away from Marcus and used his fist to pound on the driver's door. The young corporal stared back, his blue eyes dazed with disbelief. *Yeah, I get it, buddy. We never got to practice this exact scenario. Improvise and adapt!* Axel flung open the door and yanked him from his seat. "Move!" He shoved him in the direction of the mountain.

The armored truck in the middle of their convoy made a sizzling sound.

"Out! Everyone, get out!" Axel frantically waved them toward the ditch.

The occupants of the vehicle leaped and rolled from its doors only seconds before it exploded. They dove into the ditch as windows, seats, and gun parts flew everywhere.

Something hot seared Axel's shoulder blades, knocking the wind from his chest. He silently mouthed a prayer into the dirt. His foster parents hadn't been church goers, and he'd never considered himself to be a religious person, but he was beginning to understand one old saying in particular — there are no atheists in fox holes.

The screams and shouts around him gave him the energy to lift his head. More veins of fire were shooting in the direction of the third vehicle. "This way!" he bellowed, reaching for the nearest thing to wave in the air. It turned out to be a length of burning canvas. He waved it back and forth like a fiery flag, ushering the remaining soldiers into the ditch with him and his comrades. They made it a mere fraction of a second before their vehicle exploded.

He did a hasty count when the biggest pieces of carnage settled. There were only eight men. They were missing one. *Marcus!*

Axel's head spun from side to side, taking in their surroundings. "Marcus!" he shouted, low crawling from the ditch. Keeping his head down, he dragged himself by his elbows over scalding pieces of metal that burned their way through the sleeves of his uniform. Through the smoke, he could just barely make out the silhouette of their last vehicle standing — the one he and Marcus had ridden into the hellish mountain pass.

There was Marcus, up on the roof, struggling to loosen the bolts of his machine gun.

"What are you doing?" Unfortunately, the smoke had rendered Axel's voice a thick, scratchy version of its former tenor. He doubted Marcus heard him.

Understanding his friend was trying to save the weapon, but fearing he'd never be able to loosen it in time, Axel dragged himself to his knees. He reached for the bumper and pulled himself to his feet. Bullets scored the ground around him. *Great.* That meant the terrorists surrounding them were alive and well, preparing to pick off any and all American survivors like ants. It was a horrifyingly well-planned ambush. No wonder Marcus was working so hard to free the

.50 cal. They might need it to stay alive in the coming hours.

Lord, have mercy! Axel squinted up at the sky, wondering when the Air Force would arrive to launch their next strike. *Any time now would be nice.*

"Marcus!" He reached his friend and pounded on the side of the vehicle to get his attention.

Marcus either didn't hear him or chose to ignore him. Gritting his teeth, Axel swung himself up. More gunshots sounded. This time his whole body jolted from the impact. He'd been hit. How many times was hard to tell, though it felt like his left leg was on fire.

Marcus's dark gaze fastened on him in horror. "Get out!" he roared.

Axel shook his head, no longer able to speak. He extended a hand. *Not without you.* If the terrorists failed to pick them off, the vehicle was about to blow. He was surprised it had lasted this long. *Come on, brother. If I'm gonna wear that tux, we have to get out of here alive.*

More shots sounded, and Axel's other leg went numb. *Man!* He didn't dare look down.

With a roar of fury, Marcus swung the .50 cal around and opened fire in the direction of the bullets peppering their truck. Smoke billowed from beneath the hood as the flames reached them at long last.

Screaming something Axel couldn't understand, Marcus reached for Axel's arm and propelled the two of them over the side of the vehicle. Instead of heading for the ditch, however, they rolled through the dust toward the steep drop off.

The rocks and sand blurred. Axel tried to slow their progress. *This is the wrong way!* "What are you—?"

They rolled over the side of the cliff in the same second the armored truck exploded. Metal parts flew over their heads. Axel managed to grab ahold of a scraggly bush and held on, despite his fast-waning strength.

More explosions sounded — big, deep, earth-shaking ones. Much larger ones than before. They were familiar sounds, music to Axel's ears. He nearly wept with relief at the knowledge that the Air Force had finally arrived. *God bless America!* It lent him a burst of adrenaline. He used it to continue holding on, burying his face against the side of the cliff as explosion after explosion rocked both ends of the mountain pass. Debris rained down on him, but his thick kevlar shielded his head from the worst of it.

Though he couldn't feel his legs any longer, Axel felt a heavy pressure, like the mountain itself had him in its grasp and was trying to yank him loose. It was fast weakening his grip on the bush. Glancing down, he discovered the reason for the extra weight. He stared into Marcus's upturned face. The only thing in the world keeping his best friend from free-falling down the side of the cliff was his grip on Axel's ankles.

"Hold on!" Axel croaked. He feverishly struggled

to shift his weight, seeking any position that would free up one hand so he could pull Marcus to safety. *If I can hook my elbow around the bush just so...*

"Don't!" Marcus shook his head in warning. Never had his dark gaze been so full of brotherly affection... or unwavering intent. "There's no reason for us both to die today."

A chill shot through Axel's chest. *No! My God, no!*

"Semper fi." Marcus mouthed the words and let go.

Axel's mouth froze in an open-mouthed scream, though no sound emerged. Blackness clouded his vision.

The last thing he remembered were hands. Lots of hands reaching over the ledge to pull him up.

But it was too late. Marcus was already gone.

The blackness took over.

"Mister, ah...sir! Are you alright, sir?"

Axel opened his eyes to find a stewardess standing over him. Standing at his elbow was the fancily dressed Asian lady. Both were anxiously regarding him.

The stewardess was a killer blonde, maybe in her early thirties, with a pitying look in her eyes. "I've already put in a call for a wheelchair. I'm happy to ring for an ambulance, too, if—"

"No!"

She jumped at the vehemence in Axel's voice.

"No," he repeated in a gentler tone. "I am fine. Really." He pushed himself shakily to his feet. There was no way he was letting anyone roll him through the airport in a freaking wheelchair. "Got out of the hospital recently." He forced a grin he didn't feel. "They wouldn't have let me out if I wasn't ready. Trust me." His physical wounds were healed for the most part. The PTSD he was learning to live with.

"I'll make sure he gets to where he's going." With a toss of her regal head, the tiny Asian lady actually reached for Axel's sand-colored backpack that was resting in the overhead compartment.

Over my dead body! Muffling a chuckle, Axel reached up and snagged the bag, tossing it over one shoulder. He reached for her roller bag next. "I'll gladly accept your company, though. Lead the way, general."

Dark eyes twinkling, she nodded and walked ahead of him with a grace that belied her years. "I'm Aimi Kimiko, by the way. I don't believe I caught your name."

"Axel," he supplied shortly, wondering what the point was in introducing himself to a woman he'd probably never see again. "Axel Hammerstone."

"A very soldierly name." Her smile was curious.

He glanced down at his stone-washed jeans and plain black t-shirt, wondering how in heaven's name anyone could deduce from his clothing that he was a soldier.

"Dog tags," she supplied in a loud whisper with a merry glance over her shoulder.

Ah. Right. Axel eyed the unmistakable rectangular outline of the tags beneath his shirt. Though he wasn't required to wear them any more, it was turning out to be a hard habit to break after having them around his neck for the past eight years. They were all but part of his skin.

The pilot and co-pilot waited somberly in the entry way. "Thank you for your service, soldier." The pilot gave him a swift salute, and his co-pilot followed suit.

Apparently, Axel's travel companion wasn't the only one who'd noticed his dog tags.

"Ah, well, we all have our jobs." He shrugged. "Thanks for getting us to the ground in one piece." He felt a flush creep up his neck. He'd never been good at accepting compliments.

To his surprise, Mrs. Kimiko rounded on the pilot with a feisty expression riding her fine-boned features. "There was a little more bounce to the landing than I prefer, young man. I wasn't the only passenger praying that you have the sense to refill your coffee before the next flight." She winked at Axel.

The co-pilot burst out laughing and sent a playful punch in the direction of the pilot's shoulder, which inevitably reminded Axel of the easygoing banter he'd always shared with Marcus.

Ducking his head to block out the sight, he

hurried after Mrs. Kimiko. They walked side by side to the baggage claim area.

"What's next for you, Mr. Hammerstone?" she inquired in a soft, musical voice.

He had no earthly idea. "Guess I'm still figuring that out."

"You will," she returned with a conviction he didn't share.

He wished he could borrow a dose of her optimism.

"Oh, there's my granddaughter!" She raised a hand and waved it excitedly. The movement made her diamond bracelet catch the sunlight and glitter like fire.

Fire. Just the thought of fire made Axel feel the scorch of Kandahar all over again.

"You should meet her." Mrs. Kimiko shot him a sly female look from beneath her dark lashes. "She's not a soldier like you, but she's certainly in the business of protecting and serving. She's a dog handler, actually."

A dog handler? Axel's brows shot up. He failed to see how training dogs had any resemblance to being a Marine.

"Well, technically speaking, she trains search and rescue workers and their dogs how to save lives." She gave him a comical frown and swatted the air. "Kristi can explain it better than I can. How about I introduce the two of you?" She slowed her stride to stare hopefully up at him.

Axel shook his head in genuine regret. "Maybe some other time." As much as he appreciated the offer, he wasn't good company right now, and he sure as heck wasn't scouting around for a date. He had nothing to offer. No job. No home. No stability. He wasn't even sure where he was going to spend the next night.

Mrs. Kimiko nodded, though she looked disappointed. "Maybe some other time, then. I'm glad our paths crossed."

"Me, too, ma'am." He relinquished the handle of her black and gray plaid suitcase and dropped back a few steps as she hurried forward to be swept into the arms of her...

His jaw dropped. Aimi Kimiko's granddaughter was — no joke! — the most stunning woman he'd ever had the pleasure of laying eyes on. Long, dark hair with sassy, lighter brown highlights that draped nearly to her waist. She was as petite as her grandmother, but she made up for her lack of height with a pair of strappy red stilettos that accentuated the tannest, curviest legs God had ever seen fit to create. She was wearing a navy denim dress that hung just short of her knees, with a silver belt circling an impossibly tiny waist.

Even more remarkable than her beauty was the tender moment with her grandmother. After several affectionate hugs, they appeared to be talking at the same time — two people who were happy to see each other. They shared the kind of bond that only existed between families. They belonged to each other in ways Axel had never belonged to another person.

Something twisted in his chest; for a few inexplicable seconds, he would have given anything to have Aimi Kimiko's granddaughter look at him that way.

I'm an idiot. That's what Marcus would've called him for passing up the opportunity to be introduced to such a gorgeous, kindhearted woman. Marcus would already be halfway across the room. A few seconds from now, he'd have her phone number memorized.

But Axel wasn't Marcus. His limp felt a little more pronounced as he joined the latest flood of passengers disembarking from the security gates. First, he had a mound of baggage to collect. Then it would be time to figure out what came next — what was even supposed to come next.

He barely felt like putting one foot in front of the other, but Marcus had given his all so that Axel could keep marching. *I'll make your sacrifice count every day I have left, brother. This I swear!*

Hope you enjoyed the excerpt from
DISASTER CITY SEARCH AND RESCUE:
The Plus One Rescue
Available now on Amazon + FREE in KU!

Other Jo Grafford books in this series:

The Rebound One Rescue
The Fake Bride Rescue
The Blind Date Rescue
The Secret Baby Rescue
The Bridesmaid Rescue
The Girl Next Door Rescue
The Secret Crush Rescue
The Bachelorette Rescue
The Maid by Mistake Rescue
The Unlucky Bride Rescue

Much love,
Jo

SNEAK PREVIEW: HER BILLIONAIRE BOSS

A demanding billionaire boss, a marriage of convenience, and a surprise baby...

Jacey Maddox is determined to atone for her forbidden love and tragically short marriage by dedicating the rest of her career to her late husband's family firm, Genesis & Sons. That is, if they'll consider hiring a hated Maddox...

CEO Luca Calcagni is determined to teach the

rebel youngest daughter of their biggest rival the lesson of her life by hiring her as his personal assistant. He never counted on rekindling his former explosive attraction to her, any more than she counted on discovering she's carrying his late brother's baby. When she threatens to leave town and move as far as possible from the reaches of their decades-old family feud, it'll take his most skillful negotiating to maneuver her into a marriage of convenience to keep her and his last tie to his brother – her unborn child – in his life.

Except marriage to the stunningly beautiful, artistic, and complex Jacey turns out to be anything but convenient... He tries to convince himself it's only about revenge, but he can't help wondering (and secretly hoping) if her agreement to be his temporary wife could turn into his second chance at love with the only woman he's never been able to resist!

BLACK TIE BILLIONAIRES SERIES

Read them all!
Her Billionaire Boss
Her Billionaire Bodyguard
Her Billionaire Secret Admirer
Her Billionaire Best Friend
Her Billionaire Geek
Her Billionaire Double Date

BILLIONAIRE BIRTHDAY CLUB
The Billionaire's Birthday Date
The Billionaire's Birthday Blind Date
The Billionaire's Birthday Secret

Her Billionaire Boss
Available in eBook, paperback, and Kindle Unlimited!

Much love,
Jo

SNEAK PREVIEW: THE BILLIONAIRE'S BIRTHDAY DATE

Billionaire Birthday Club

What do you give a billionaire who already has everything?

Roman Cantona is promoted to CEO of his family's hotel conglomerate. He always knew this day would come; he just never imagined it would come so tragically or so quickly. There are too many things he never had the opportunity to cross off his bucket list before shouldering the weight of the Cantona dynasty, and now he has time for little else besides work. As his birthday approaches, he's in no mood to celebrate. At the last minute, however, he accepts a friend's dare to submit an application for an exclusive birthday experience…or so the website claims.

Rising pop singer Celine Petrova receives an invitation from an exotic resort for a weekend singing tour. Though she's preparing for her graduate thesis project, she can't afford to turn down the opportunity. She is shocked to come face-to-face with the man who funded her full-ride scholarship — the very hunky, very sweet billionaire who looks like he could use some cheering up...

One-click this sweet and clean billionaire romance, and be whisked into a world of glamor, boardroom intrigue, and happily-ever-afters!

BILLIONAIRE BIRTHDAY CLUB is an exclusive retreat — for the billionaire who appears to have everything but secretly wants more. After filling out a confidential survey, a curated celebration is waiting on the island to make all his birthday wishes come true!

BILLIONAIRE BIRTHDAY CLUB TITLES BY JO

The Billionaire's Birthday Date
The Billionaire's Birthday Blind Date
The Billionaire's Birthday Secret
Available in eBook and paperback on Amazon + FREE in Kindle Unlimited!

Much love,
Jo

READ MORE JO

Jo is an Amazon bestselling author of sweet and inspirational romance stories with humor, heart, and happily-ever-afters.

Free Book!

Visit www.JoGrafford.com to sign up for Jo's New Release Newsletter and receive a FREE copy of one of her sweet romance stories!

1.) Follow on Amazon!
amazon.com/author/jografford

2.) Join Cuppa Jo Readers!
https://www.facebook.com/groups/CuppaJoReaders

3.) Join Heroes and Hunks Readers!
https://www.facebook.com/groups/HeroesandHunks/

4.) Follow on Bookbub!
https://www.bookbub.com/authors/jo-grafford

5.) Follow on Instagram!
https://www.instagram.com/jografford/

- amazon.com/authors/jo-grafford
- bookbub.com/authors/jo-grafford
- facebook.com/jografford
- twitter.com/jografford
- instagram.com/jografford
- pinterest.com/jografford

ALSO BY JO GRAFFORD

Visit www.JoGrafford.com to sign up for Jo's New Release Newsletter and to receive your FREE copy of one of her sweet romance stories!

Born In Texas: Hometown Heroes A-Z

written exclusively by Jo Grafford

The whole alphabet is coming!

A - Accidental Hero

B - Best Friend Hero

C - Celebrity Hero

D - Damaged Hero

E - Enemies to Hero

Disaster City Search and Rescue

(a multi-author series)

Titles by Jo:

The Rebound Rescue

The Plus One Rescue

The Blind Date Rescue

The Fake Bride Rescue
The Secret Baby Rescue
The Bridesmaid Rescue
The Girl Next Door Rescue
The Secret Crush Rescue
The Bachelorette Rescue
The Maid By Mistake Rescue
The Unlucky Bride Rescue

Black Tie Billionaires
written exclusively by Jo Grafford
Her Billionaire Champion — a Prequel
Her Billionaire Boss
Her Billionaire Bodyguard
Her Billionaire Secret Admirer
Her Billionaire Best Friend
Her Billionaire Geek
Her Billionaire Double Date

Heart Lake
written exclusively by Jo Grafford
Winds of Change
Song of Nightingales

Perils of Starlight

Billionaire Birthday Club
(a multi-author series)
Titles by Jo:
The Billionaire's Birthday Date
The Billionaire's Birthday Blind Date
The Billionaire's Birthday Secret
Billionaire Birthday Club Box Set

Mail Order Brides Rescue Series
written exclusively by Jo Grafford
Hot-Tempered Hannah
Cold-Feet Callie
Fiery Felicity
Misunderstood Meg
Dare-Devil Daisy
Outrageous Olivia
Jinglebell Jane
Absentminded Amelia
Bookish Belinda
Tenacious Trudy
Meddlesome Madge

Mismatched MaryAnne

MOB Rescue Series Box Set Books 1-4

MOB Rescue Series Box Set Books 5-8

MOB Rescue Series Box Set Books 9-12

Mail Order Brides of Christmas Mountain

written exclusively by Jo Grafford

Bride for the Innkeeper

Bride for the Deputy

Bride for the Tribal Chief

Angel Creek Christmas Brides

(a multi-author series)

Titles by Jo:

Elizabeth

Grace

Lilly

Once Upon a Church House Series

written exclusively by Jo Grafford

Abigail

Rachel

Naomi

Esther

The Lawkeepers

(a multi-author series)

Titles by Jo:

Lawfully Ours

Lawfully Loyal

Lawfully Witnessed

Lawfully Brave

Lawfully Courageous

Widows, Brides, and Secret Babies

(a multi-author series)

Titles by Jo:

Mail Order Mallory

Mail Order Isabella

Mail Order Melissande

Christmas Rescue Series

(a multi-author series)

Title by Jo:

Rescuing the Blacksmith

Border Brides

(a multi-author Series)

Titles by Jo:

Wild Rose Summer

Going All In

Herd the Heavens

The Pinkerton Matchmaker

(a multi-author series)

Titles by Jo:

An Agent for Bernadette

An Agent for Lorelai

An Agent for Jolene

An Agent for Madeleine

Lost Colony Series

written exclusively by Jo Grafford

Breaking Ties

Trail of Crosses

Into the Mainland

Higher Tides

―――

Ornamental Match Maker Series

(a multi-author series)

Titles by Jo:

Angel Cookie Christmas

Star-Studded Christmas

Stolen Heart Valentine

Miracle for Christmas in July

Home for Christmas

―――

Whispers In Wyoming

(a multi-author series)

Titles by Jo:

His Wish, Her Command

His Heart, Her Love

―――

Silverpines

(a multi-author series)

Titles by Jo:

Wanted: Bounty Hunter

The Bounty Hunter's Sister

―――

Brides of Pelican Rapids

(a multi-author series)

Title by Jo:

Rebecca's Dream

―――

Sailors and Saints

(a multi-author series)

Title by Jo:

The Sailor and the Surgeon

Made in the USA
Middletown, DE
13 October 2021